BOOK**SHOTS**

AVAILABLE NOW!

CROSS KILL

Along Came a Spider killer Gary Soneji died years ago. But Alex Cross swears he sees Soneji gun down his partner. Is his greatest enemy back from the grave?

ZOO II

Humans are evolving into a savage new species that could save civilization— or end it. James Patterson's *Zoo* was just the beginning.

UPCOMING TITLES

THE TRIAL

An accused killer will do anything to disrupt his own trial, including a courtroom shocker that Lindsay Boxer and the Women's Murder Club will never see coming.

LITTLE BLACK DRESS

Can a little black dress change everything? What begins as one woman's fantasy is about to go too far.

LET'S PLAY MAKE-BELIEVE

Christy and Marty just met, and it's love at first sight. Or is it? One of them is playing a dangerous game—and only one will survive.

CHASE

A man falls to his death in an apparent accident. But why does he have a dead man's fingerprints? Detective Michael Bennett is on the case.

HUNTED

Someone is luring men from the streets to play a mysterious, high-stakes game. Former Special Forces officer David Shelley goes undercover to shut it down—but will he win?

$10,000,000 MARRIAGE PROPOSAL

A mysterious billboard offering $10 million to get married intrigues three single women in LA. But who is Mr. Right…and is he the perfect match for the lucky winner?

THE FRENCH KISS

It's hard enough to move to a new city, but now everyone French detective Luc Moncrief cares about is being killed off. Welcome to New York.

KILLER CHEF

Caleb Rooney knows how to do two things: run a food truck and solve a murder. When people suddenly start dying of foodborne illnesses, the stakes are higher than ever.…

113 MINUTES

Molly Rourke's son has been murdered. Now she'll do whatever it takes to get justice. No one should underestimate a mother's love.…

THE CHRISTMAS MYSTERY

Two stolen paintings disappear from a Park Avenue murder scene—French detective Luc Moncrief is in for a merry Christmas.

BLACK & BLUE

Detective Harry Blue is determined to take down the serial killer who's abducted several women, but her mission leads to a shocking revelation.

James Patterson's
BOOK SH⬥TS
Flames

UPCOMING ROMANCES

LEARNING TO RIDE

City girl Madeline Harper never wanted to love a cowboy. But rodeo king Tanner Callen might change her mind…and win her heart.

THE MCCULLAGH INN IN MAINE

Chelsea O'Kane escapes to Maine to build a new life—until she runs into Jeremy Holland, an old flame.…

SACKING THE QUARTERBACK

Attorney Melissa St. James wins every case. Now, when she's defending football superstar Grayson Knight, her heart is on the line too.

DAZZLING—THE DIAMOND TRILOGY, PART I

To support her artistic career, Siobhan Dempsey works at the elite Stone Room in New York City…never expecting to be swept away by Derick Miller.

RADIANT—THE DIAMOND TRILOGY, PART II

After an explosive breakup with her billionaire boyfriend, Siobhan moves to Detroit to pursue her art. But Derick isn't ready to give her up.

BODYGUARD

Special Agent Abbie Whitmore has only one task: protect Congressman Jonathan Lassiter from a violent cartel's threats. Yet she's never had to do it while falling in love.…

"ALEX CROSS, I'M COMING FOR YOU...."

Gary Soneji, the killer from *Along Came a Spider,* has been dead for more than ten years—but Cross swears he saw Soneji gun down his partner. Is Cross's worst enemy back from the grave?

Nothing will prepare you for the wicked truth.

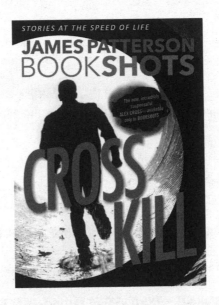

Read the next riveting, pulse-racing Alex Cross adventure, available only in

BOOK**SHOTS**

"I'M NOT ON TRIAL. SAN FRANCISCO IS."

Drug cartel boss the Kingfisher has a reputation for being violent and merciless. And after he's finally caught, he's set to stand trial for his vicious crimes—until he begins unleashing chaos and terror upon the lawyers, jurors, and police associated with the case. The city is paralyzed, and Detective Lindsay Boxer is caught in the eye of the storm.

Will the Women's Murder Club make it out alive—or will a sudden courtroom snare ensure their last breaths?

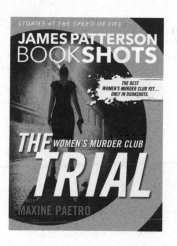

Read the new Women's Murder Club story, out on July 5, available only in

BOOK**SHOTS**

ZOO II

JAMES PATTERSON
WITH MAX DILALLO

BOOK**SHOTS**

Little, Brown and Company

New York Boston London

BookShots / Little, Brown and Company
Hachette Book Group
1290 Avenue of the Americas, New York, NY 10104
bookshots.com

First Edition: June 2016

BookShots is an imprint of Little, Brown and Company, a division of Hachette Book Group, Inc. The Little, Brown name and logo are trademarks of Hachette Book Group, Inc. The BookShots name and logo are a trademark of JBP Business, LLC.

The publisher is not responsible for websites (or their content) that are not owned by the publisher.

The Hachette Speakers Bureau provides a wide range of authors for speaking events. To find out more, go to hachettespeakersbureau.com or call (866) 376-6591.

ISBN 978-0-316-31712-2
LCCN 2016934158

10 9 8 7 6 5 4 3 2 1

RRD-C

Printed in the United States of America

ZOO II

CHAPTER 1

I'M RUNNING FOR MY LIFE.

At least I'm trying to.

My clunky rubber boots keep getting stuck in the fresh snowfall. Fifty-mile-per-hour Arctic winds lash my body like a palm tree in a hurricane. The subzero-weather hooded jumpsuit I'm wearing is more cumbersome than a suit of armor.

Mini-icicles crust my goggles. Not that I could see much through them, anyway. All around me is a wall of white, a vortex of icy gusts and swirling snow. I can't even make out my triple-gloved right hand in front of my face.

But that's because it's tucked into my front pocket, clutching a Glock 17 9mm pistol. My one and only hope of survival.

I keep moving—"stumbling" would be more accurate—as fast as I can. I don't know where the hell I'm going. I just know I have to get there fast. I know I can't stop.

If I do, the seven-hundred-pound female polar bear on my tail will catch me and devour me alive.

But, hey, that's life above the Arctic Circle for you. Never a dull moment. One second you're tossing a net into an icy stream, trying to catch a few fish to feed your family. The next, one of Earth's deadliest predators is trying to kill you.

I glance backward to try to see just how close the bear has gotten. I can't spot her at all, which is even more terrifying. With all the snow swirling around, her milky-white coat makes the perfect camouflage.

But I know the animal is near. I can just feel it.

Sure enough, seconds later, from behind me comes a mighty roar that echoes out across the tundra.

She's closer than I thought!

I push myself to move faster and tighten my grip around the freezing-cold Glock, wishing I had a larger gun. Do I empty my clip at the bear blindly and hope I get lucky? Stop, crouch, wait for her to get nearer, and aim for maximum effect?

Neither sounds promising. So I decide to do both.

Without slowing, I turn sideways and fire four times in her general direction.

Did I hit her? No clue. I'm sure I didn't scare her. Unlike most animals, typical polar bears never get spooked by loud noises. They live in the Arctic, after all. They hear thunderous sounds all the time: rumbling avalanches, shattering glaciers.

But there's nothing typical about this polar bear whatsoever. I didn't provoke her. I didn't wander into her territory. I didn't threaten her young.

None of that matters. She wants me dead.

The reason? HAC. Human-animal conflict. My theory that has helped explain why, for the past half-dozen years, animals everywhere have been waging an all-out war against humanity—and winning. It's why this abominable snow-bear picked up my scent from over a mile away and immediately started charging. I'm a human being and, like every other animal on the planet right now, she has an insatiable craving for human blood.

Another roar booms behind me, revealing the bear's position—even closer now.

I twist to fire off four more rounds. I pray I've hit her, but I don't count on it. With only nine bullets in my clip remaining, I start psyching myself up to turn around, kneel, and take aim.

Okay, Oz, I think. *You can do this. You can—*

I suddenly lose my footing and go tumbling face-first onto the icy ground. It's hard as concrete and jagged as a bed of nails. My gun—*shit!*—goes flying out of my hand and into a snowdrift.

I scramble on all fours and hunt for it desperately, feeling the permafrost beneath me start to tremble from the polar bear's galloping gait.

I could really use that gun right about now.

By the grace of God, I find it just in time. I spin around—right as the bear emerges from the white haze like a speeding train bursting out of a tunnel.

She rears up onto her hind legs, preparing to pounce. I fire four more shots. The first hits the side of her thick skull—but ricochets clean off. The next two miss her completely. The fourth lodges in her shoulder, which only makes her madder.

I shoot twice more, wildly, as I try to roll away, but the bear leaps and lands right on top of me. She chomps down on my snowsuit hood with her mighty jaws, missing my skull by millimeters. She jerks me around like a rag doll. With her razor-sharp claws, she slashes my left arm to shreds.

Pain surges through my limb as I twist and struggle, trying to break free with every ounce of strength I have. Images of Chloe and Eli, my wife and young son, flash through my mind. I can't leave them. I can't die. Not now. Not like this.

I'm still getting tossed around like crazy, but with all the strength I can muster, I shove the tip of my Glock against the bottom of the polar bear's chin, just inches from my own.

I fire my last three shots point-blank.

A mist of hot blood sprays my face as the bullets tear through the behemoth's brain. She stops moving instantly, as if she were a toy and I'd just flipped her off switch. Then all seven hundred pounds of her slump down next to me.

Seconds pass and I begin to catch my breath, relieved beyond belief. Slowly, with all my effort, I reach up and manage to pry my hood from the bear's locked jaw.

I stagger to my feet, instantly light-headed from the adrenaline crash. Or maybe it's the blood loss. My left arm is gushing from easily a dozen lacerations.

Removing the polar-bear-blood-soaked goggles from my face, I survey the massive animal that nearly took my life. Even dead she's a terrifying sight. *Unbelievable.*

I thought my family and I would be safe up here. That's the whole reason we're living in Greenland in the first place, to avoid the sheer hell of constant deadly animal attacks. So much for *that*.

I just have to remind myself: the rest of the world is even worse.

CHAPTER 2

"YOU COULD HAVE DIED out there, Oz! What the hell were you thinking?"

My wife, Chloe Tousignant, paces the cramped quarters of our tiny galley kitchen, anxiously twisting the cuffs of her thick wool sweater, biting her bottom lip.

Chloe's furious with me, and I don't blame her. But I have to admit, I've forgotten how awfully sexy she looks when she's mad. Even scared or angry, my French-born wife is both the most beautiful and most brilliant woman I've ever met.

"Come on, how many times are you going to ask me that?"

This would be number six, for those of you keeping track at home.

The first was when I came stumbling back inside covered in blood—the polar bear's and my own. The second: when Chloe was helping me clean and dress my wounds. The third was when I went back outside again, the fourth when I returned dragging as much of the carcass as I could. The fifth was while she watched me butcher it. (I *think,* but I was focusing pretty intently on the YouTube video I was watching, via our spotty satellite internet connection: *How to Skin a Bear ~ A Guide for First-Time Hunters.*)

"I just don't understand!" she exclaims. "How could you—"

"Shh, keep your voice down," I say gently, gesturing to the tiny room right next to us, where our four-year-old son, Eli, is taking a nap.

Chloe frowns and switches to a harsh whisper. "How could you take such a risk? It was completely unnecessary! You know it's prime mating season all across the tundra. The animals are even crazier than normal. And we still have plenty of food left."

I take a moment to weigh my response.

The reality is, we *don't* have plenty of food left. We've been living in this abandoned Arctic weather station for nearly four months now. Originally settled at Thule Air Base, twenty-five miles away, with President Hardinson and a group of government officials, we had been on our own since they returned to the United States to manage the animal crisis more closely.

Chloe and I had decided to stay. We thought it would be safer. We hoped that living in such a harsh climate, home to fewer wild animals, would mean fewer wild animal *attacks*. And for the most part, it did. It also meant we were left to our own devices.

Yes, Chloe is right that it's prime mating season—because it's late "summer" and, relatively speaking, fairly temperate. But even colder, more brutal weather is just around the corner. Every day I don't go out there and trap a wild caribou or haul in some fresh fish to tide us over through winter threatens our survival.

As I stand over our little propane stove, stirring a gigantic pot of simmering polar bear stew, I decide to keep all of that to myself. Instead, I extend an olive branch.

"You're right, honey. It was pretty dumb of me. I'm sorry."

Chloe probably knows I'm just trying to play nice. A highly educated scientist, she's well aware of the Arctic's weather patterns. And I can guarantee that, as a deeply devoted mother, she's been keeping a worried eye on our rations. Still, she clearly appreciates my words.

"I'm just glad you brought that gun along," she says.

"Are you kidding? That thing's like American Express. I never leave my three-room Arctic hut without it."

Chloe laughs, grateful for a little comic relief. Which makes me feel happy, too. There's no better feeling in the world than being able to make her smile.

She comes up behind me and nuzzles my neck. I wince as she brushes against my bad arm, the bloody slash wounds throbbing beneath the bandages.

"Sorry," she says, backing off. "The pain must be awful."

It is. But Chloe's got enough on her mind. I don't want her worrying about me.

I turn around to face her. Her concern, her love, her beauty are all too much.

"Not too bad," I reply. "But maybe you can help me…forget about it for a while?"

She coyly arches an eyebrow. We start to kiss. Before long, things are heating up faster than the polar bear meat cooking behind me.

Until Chloe suddenly stops. She pulls away. "Wait. Oz, we can't."

I sigh, disappointed. But she's right. Stranded deep inside the Arctic Circle, there's not exactly a corner drugstore we can run to for some condoms or the Pill.

I simply nod and hug her. Tightly.

This isn't a world that either of us would risk bringing new life into.

CHAPTER 3

"YUCK! DADDY, THIS IS GROSS!"

Eli has just taken his first bite of my latest culinary creation: oatmeal mixed with chunks of braised polar bear. He spits it back out into his bowl.

Chloe folds her arms. "Eli, where are your manners?"

How adorably French of her, I think. The world is falling apart and my wife is still concerned about etiquette.

"Oh, go easy on him," I say. "I know it's not exactly the breakfast of champions. But you do have to eat it, buddy. Sorry. We all do. Need the protein."

"No way," Eli says, shaking his head. He proceeds to shovel only the mushy oatmeal into his mouth, avoiding the meat. He uses his fingers, not his spoon.

I don't have the energy to put up a fight, and neither does Chloe. We consume the rest of our meal in silence. All we can hear is the eerie, howling wind outside, whipping against our weather station's aluminum walls. It sounds like something right out of a horror movie.

At least it's not an animal, trying to claw its way inside. It might be soon.

Chloe and I had come to the same chilling conclusion the night before. Because I lost so much blood out there on the ice, leaving a trail leading right to our front door, it's only a matter of time before *other* creatures pick up the scent and come after us. Like a charging herd of enraged musk oxen. Or a throng of feral foxes. Another polar bear, or an entire pack of them.

"All right, who's ready for story time?" Chloe asks, starting to clear our plates.

"Me, me!" Eli shouts, his face lighting up bright.

"Okay, then. Go wash your hands and get ready. I'll be in in a minute."

With a grin practically half the size of his face, Eli disappears into the other room.

When we first moved into the weather station, it was all so rushed and chaotic. Our main focus was making sure we had enough canned food and warm clothing. Toys, games, and books for Eli were the last things on our mind. Thankfully, we discovered the previous inhabitants were voracious readers. They'd left behind a giant library—everything from Charles Dickens to Philip K. Dick, though not exactly young children's literature. Still, Chloe and I have been reading selections to Eli every single day since. Most of the stuff is way over his head, but he loves it.

"Anything new in the world we left behind?" Chloe asks me, rinsing our plates.

She sees I've started skimming the *New York Times* homepage on my laptop. More than half the lead headlines are about the ongoing animal crisis, which shows no signs of slowing down. In fact, it's only getting worse.

I summarize some stories.

"Let's see. Researchers in Cameroon were testing a promising animal pheromone repellent spray when they were mauled by a horde of rhinos. President Hardinson just signed a controversial executive order to set controlled fires in federal parks to destroy thousands of acres of breeding grounds. And the Kremlin's denying it, but apparently a school of blue whales just sunk a Russian nuclear submarine in—"

"Enough!" Chloe snaps. She sighs deeply. She runs her hands through her auburn hair. I feel bad for adding to her stress, but she asked.

My laptop *pings* with a notification—a new email. But not just any message—this has been sent via a classified U.S. government server.

Its subject line reads: "Urgent Request."

I immediately slam my laptop shut.

"Now don't be ridiculous," Chloe says. She'd read the screen over my shoulder. "Open it, Oz. It must be important!"

"As far as I'm concerned," I say, "there are only two things in this crazy world that are important—and they're both inside this weather station with me. I'm done helping the feds, thank you very much. Remember what happened last time? How royally they screwed everything up with their so-called solutions? The idiotic bombing raids? The bungled electricity ban?"

Chloe puts her hands on her hips. Of course she remembers. We lived through every minute of that nightmare together.

But then she snatches my computer away.

"Fine. If you're not going to read it, I will."

She opens the laptop and clicks on the message. She begins to skim it, and I can see her eyes grow wide. Whatever she's reading is big. Very big.

"Let me guess. The Pentagon wants me to come back and try to help solve this thing again. But what's the point? They're not going to listen to me."

Chloe spins the screen around and shows me the email. I read it myself.

It was sent by a Dr. Evan Freitas, undersecretary for science and energy at the DOE. He explains that the powers that be in Washington have finally acknowledged that the animal crisis must be dealt with scientifically, *not* militarily. The Department of Energy is now overseeing America's response, not the Department of Defense. Dr. Freitas is spearheading the new response team personally, and he desperately wants me, Jackson Oz, renowned human-animal conflict expert, to return to the United States and join it.

"This is our chance," Chloe says, grabbing my shoulders, "to get out of this icy hell. To actually stop this thing this time. It's what we've been waiting for!"

I can see tears forming in the corners of my wife's big brown eyes. It's obvious how much this means to her. I'm still skeptical, but I know I can't refuse.

"You're right," I finally reply. "It is what we've been waiting for. It's hope."

CHAPTER 4

THE METAL WALLS OF our little weather station are rattling like a tin can. Outside, something's rumbling, something big. And it's getting louder. Closer.

"Daddy, look!" Eli exclaims. He's standing in front of a triple-paned glass window that looks out across the icy tundra, jabbing his finger at the sky. "It's here!"

The rumbling grows to a crescendo as a gunmetal military transport plane roars overhead, flying dangerously low to the ground.

Which is a very beautiful sight. It means it's about to land. Right on time.

As it touches down—on the snow-covered airstrip about a quarter-mile from our hut—Chloe and I quickly gather up the few small duffel bags we'll be bringing with us. Mostly clothes, toiletries, and a dog-eared copy of *A Tale of Two Cities* we're halfway through reading to Eli.

Other than the hooded jumpsuits we're already wearing, we're leaving the rest of our extreme cold-weather gear behind. I'd started packing our thermal underwear last night, until Chloe saw me and practically slapped the long johns out of my hand.

"I hope you're joking," she said, crossing her arms. "We're done living in this damned Arctic wasteland. Forever. We're returning to civilization, remember? And we're *saving* it. For real this time."

"Right," I said. "Of course." Then, under my breath: "No pressure or anything."

But my wife had a point. We'd decided to leave our safe little hide-out at the edge of the world. We both knew there would be no coming back.

"Okay, bud, time to go," I call to Eli, who eagerly jumps into Chloe's arms.

We assemble by the front door, which we haven't opened in nearly a week—not since I tangled with that polar bear and left a trail of her blood and mine right to our doorstep. Chloe and I were afraid more wild animals would pick up the scent and come calling.

By the evening of the next day, they had.

First was a herd of rabid reindeer. They rammed their hoofs and antlers against the metal siding for hours until finally giving up from exhaustion. Next came a pack of wolverines. Not the scary Hugh Jackman mutant kind but weasel-like critters the size of small dogs. Still, their teeth and claws are as sharp as razors. If they'd found a way in, they'd have had no trouble turning three helpless humans into mincemeat.

I peer through the door's porthole. The coast looks clear—but anything could be out there. Lurking. Waiting. The quarter-mile hike to the airstrip might as well be a marathon.

Which is why I'm holding that trusty Glock—the one that saved my life once before—just in case. I check the clip: seventeen shiny gold bullets. Locked and loaded.

I push open the door and the three of us step outside. With my very first breath, the frigid air stabs the back of my throat like a knife.

"Come on," I manage to croak. "Let's hurry."

We traipse as fast as we can across the fresh snow; it's up to our knees. Over the crunching of our footsteps and the whistling of the wind, I hear Chloe speaking some comforting words to our son to help keep him calm.

Meanwhile, I'm scanning the icy vista all around us like a hawk. Which is harder than you might think. The endless snow and ice reflect the midday sun brighter than a million mirrors. If a feral animal or two—or ten—came charging toward us, sure, I'd probably spot them in time. But would I be able to see well enough in the glare to aim and fire?

I pray I don't have to find out.

Before long I do spot something looming. It's bluish-gray. And enormous.

It's the C-12 Huron transport plane—its dual propellers still spinning—sent by the Air Force to take us home.

We finally reach it as its rear stairs are hydraulically lowered. I gesture for Chloe and Eli to board first. I take one final glance around, say a silent good-bye to this icy hell, then climb in after them.

"IDs and boarding passes, please?"

One of the two pilots, a surprisingly youngish woman with a megawatt grin, is turned around in her seat to face us. Chloe and I smile back, filled with relief and glad to discover our saviors have a sense of humor.

"Shoot," I say, patting my pockets. "I think I left my wallet in my other subzero bodysuit."

"I'm Major Schiff," the captain says, grinning. "This is First Lieutenant Kimmel. Sit down, strap in, and let's get you guys out of here."

There are only about a dozen plush leather seats in the plane, which we have all to ourselves. Eli picks one by the window. Chloe sits next to him, and I beside her.

Within seconds, the plane's engines come alive and we're speeding down the bumpy, potholed runway. As we lift off into the sky, I close my eyes for just a moment…

When I hear Eli shriek at the top of his lungs.

"Look, look!" He's pointing out the window. A flock of birds—looks like a mix of gulls and ducks and even owls—has suddenly appeared on the horizon, flying right at us. They can't touch a speeding jet, and we leave the squawking mass of feathers in our atmospheric dust.

I reach over and take Chloe's hand. It's clammy. And trembling.

I realize mine is, too.

CHAPTER 5

THE PLANE'S CABIN IS pitch-black. We've been flying for hours. Eli and Chloe are snoring softly, both sleeping like babies.

Me? Not even close.

I'm exhausted but haven't caught a wink. My first stop, before returning to the United States, is London. There I'll attend an international summit to discuss new global responses to the animal attacks with representatives from around the world.

My mind's been on overdrive pretty much since wheels-up. That world we're returning to after all this time—what does it look like? The government's promise to treat HAC as a scientific crisis, not a military one—how will that actually play out? And what is my role in it all?

The lights inside the cabin come on. Major Schiff turns to face me.

"Time to stow those tray tables. We're about to land."

Now my heart rate really starts to rise. Not because of the summit in London.

No, I'm getting nervous because we're *not* landing in London right now.

And my wife has no idea yet.

Chloe rubs her eyes and sits up in her seat. She gives me a groggy smile and glances out the window—when her expression instantly turns to shock. Then anger.

"Oz…? Where are we?"

She asks rhetorically, of course. We've just flown past the Eiffel Tower.

"Chloe, look, I'm sorry. If I'd told you the truth—"

"I never would have agreed to it, you're absolutely right!"

"Listen, I can explain—"

"No, let *me*," she fires back. "While you jet off to London for the conference, then to God-knows-where-else around the world, Eli and I will be staying here. In Paris. With my parents. Because in your head you've convinced yourself that's safer!"

Chloe knows me too well. That was my plan to a T. I'd arranged it secretly with Dr. Freitas of the Department of Energy. And it did sound good in my head. But hearing my wife repeat it back to me, I can't help but wonder if I've done the right thing.

"If there was any way we could stay together," I say, "any way at all, you know I'd choose that in a heartbeat. But be real, Chloe. Let's say they send me to the Amazon. Or Mount Kilimanjaro. Or the *Ant*arctic. Are those any places to take a four-year-old?"

Chloe just rolls her beautiful eyes.

I want to tell her we'll talk every day, no matter where in the world I am. I want her to know that every second I'm not working on solving the animal crisis, I'll be thinking about her and Eli. I want her to believe me when I promise I'll be coming back to get them as soon as I possibly can.

But I don't get a chance to say any of that. Our plane touches down on a private runway at Le Bourget, and before I know it, Chloe and I are walking down the retractable steps, Eli in my arms. A shiny black Citroën sedan and a handful of people are already waiting for us on the tarmac.

"Chloe, *ma petite chérie!*"

Marielle Tousignant, my wife's bubbly seventy-year-old step-mother, wraps her in an emotional hug. Marielle married her widowed father when Chloe was still fairly young. She never adopted Chloe officially, but it didn't matter. Marielle couldn't have children of her own, and before long, the two became extremely close, as if biological relatives.

I stand in silence as they speak to each other in rapid-fire French. I can't understand a word, but the gist of their conversation is pretty obvious.

"*Salut,* Oz," Marielle says to me, kissing both my cheeks and blotting her eyes. "Thank you for returning to me my daughter."

"Of course, Marielle," I say. "Thanks for taking care of her while I'm gone."

"And who is this handsome *garçon?*" she asks, gently stroking sleeping Eli's hair.

Chloe furrows her brow. Is her stepmother making a joke? Or is it something else?

"Very funny, *Maman,*" she says. "That's your grandson."

After the slightest pause, an embarrassed smile blooms across Marielle's face. "*Oui, bien sûr!* My, how big Eli is getting!"

A suited man standing by the car interrupts us: "Ma'am?"

He has an American accent, and I presume he's one of the U.S. Embassy security escorts Dr. Freitas promised would pick Chloe and Eli up from the airport. "We should get going."

Everyone agrees. Eli is still sleeping, and as Chloe takes him gently from me, I can tell from her expression she's still upset. Is it because I didn't tell her the plan? Because we're going to be apart again? Or because the world has come to this?

Probably all three.

"Where's Papa?" I hear her ask Marielle as we approach the sedan.

"Right here, my dear," comes a scratchy old voice from inside the vehicle.

Jean-Luc Tousignant, my wife's seventy-six-year-old father, is sitting in the backseat. A wooden cane is draped across his knees. As he reaches up to embrace his daughter, his hands tremble terribly.

"Forgive me for not getting out. I do not have the strength."

Chloe can barely hide her shock. Neither can I. The last time we saw him, just a year ago, when he and Marielle visited us in New York, Jean-Luc, a former French Foreign Legion officer, was hale and hearty for his age. Tonight he looks frail and sick.

Wonderful, I think. I figured my wife and son would be safe in Paris with my in-laws. I had no idea that one of them had developed early-stage dementia and the other, Parkinson's.

But at least this is safer than bringing Chloe and Eli with me to dangerous, far-flung lands…right?

I suddenly feel my wife pressing up against me, her arms around my neck, her lips on mine.

"I hate you so much, Oz," she whispers between kisses. "But I love you more."

I tell her I love her, too. I tell her to be safe. To watch over Eli. That I'll be back for them.

"Just as soon as I save the world. *I promise.*"

With that, Chloe gets into the sedan and it speeds away into the night.

As I climb back up the steps of the plane, I swallow the growing lump in my throat. I knew saying good-bye to my family wasn't going to be easy.

Now comes the even harder part.

CHAPTER 6

DAWN IS BREAKING OVER London. It's 2016, but squint, and you'd swear it was back during the Blitz.

Our three-SUV convoy is speeding east along Marylebone Road, one of the city's central thoroughfares. My eyes are glued to the streetscape outside the window, and my jaw is stuck to the floor. I'm getting my first glimpse of just how much the world has changed since I've been gone.

By "changed," I mean "gone to absolute shit."

The sidewalks are splattered with dried blood and strewn with debris and broken glass. Gutters are filled with soggy garbage. Shops are boarded up. Most traffic lights are out. A few other cars and trucks are on the road—police and military vehicles, generally—but I don't see a single pedestrian.

Instead, central London is overrun by animals—in particular, roving packs of rangy, rabid wolves.

Their fur is patchy, but their fangs glisten like icicles. They seem to be stalking down virtually every sidewalk and alley we pass, sniffing the ground, searching for human prey.

Clearly they're the primary animal threat in this part of the city.

But I also spot plenty of feral dogs and house cats in the mix. I see squirrels skittering across rooftops, too. A flock of falcons circling and cawing overhead.

When we pass a burnt-out black London cab, abandoned on the corner of Baker Street—near the address of the fictional Sherlock Holmes—I notice that inside, about fifty greasy rats have built a giant, filthy nest. They're gnawing the flesh off a severed human leg, and it doesn't take a crack detective to figure out how they got it.

"Welcome back to the jungle, Oz."

Seated beside me, Dr. Evan Freitas pats me on the shoulder and lets out a grim chuckle. He can't be more than fifty, but the stress of spearheading Washington's scientific HAC response has clearly aged him prematurely. His bushy black beard is streaked with gray. Every time he speaks, his entire face fills with wrinkles like a prune.

"It's...it's just...," I stutter, "unbelievable."

"Worse than you imagined?"

"Worse than—my worst *nightmare!* We had satellite internet back in the Arctic. I'd read that the animals were gaining ground. That huge swaths of major cities had basically been overrun. And abandoned. But this...this is just beyond—"

"London Town ain't been abandoned, mate," says Jack Riley, our driver, a cranky, baldheaded Brit with the Metropolitan Police. "See?"

He gestures to an apartment above what was once a high-end shoe store, now looted and dark. A woman has opened her second-story window a crack. She quickly reels in a line of laundry and slams the window shut.

"The whole bloody lot of us just stay indoors now. Least the smart ones do."

Yep, I'd read about that as well.

In many places, just setting foot onto the street is a death wish. So most people, especially in big cities, remain inside their homes pretty much 24/7, with their doors and windows locked tight. Some have gone even further, converting their buildings into anti-animal mini-fortresses, as Chloe's parents and a few neighbors had done to their Paris apartment complex. It was one of the many reasons I thought my wife and son would be safer there.

Folks communicate with friends and family almost exclusively by phone and internet—even more so than they did before. School and work are done online as much as possible. In terms of food and other necessities, people have come to rely on sporadic deliveries of rations by armed government soldiers. Doctors have gone back to making house calls, at great personal risk…and are almost always packing heat.

"It's like this in Atlanta, too. And the suburbs and surrounding counties? Even worse. People are getting desperate. Civilization is breaking down."

Those ominous words come from the woman sitting in the row of seats behind us, nervously biting her cuticles: Dr. Sarah Lipchitz.

While I'd waited with Freitas at Heathrow for about half an hour for Sarah's plane to arrive from the United States, he explained that she was a brilliant young biologist and pathogen expert currently employed by the Centers for Disease Control and Prevention, who had been handpicked to join our team. (What he *didn't* mention was that the bespectacled Sarah was very pretty, in a geeky, girl-next-door kind of way.)

"Precisely, Doctor," Freitas responds. "And preventing global chaos from becoming total anarchy is why we're all here."

He means me, Sarah, himself, and the rest of the scientists and experts in our three-vehicle convoy. Barely a dozen people, responsible for the lives of millions.

I have about a thousand follow-up questions for Freitas, but they'll have to wait. We pass Hampstead Road and turn down a one-way side street. Our convoy comes to a stop in front of the main gates of University College London. The international symposium we've come to England to attend is a gathering of some of the finest scientific minds in the world, all trying to save humanity.

As armed British soldiers open our doors and escort us inside, I hear a pack of wolves in the distance, howling.

I hope they're not signaling that another innocent person has been mauled.

CHAPTER 7

MY GOD, THESE SCIENTIFIC conferences are dull.

I'd forgotten how absolutely painful they can be. Even when the topic is literally the fate of the planet, the only thing these bland professors and rumpled "experts" seem to know how to do is drone on and on. And on.

It makes me want to pull my hair out. Worst of all, we've been at this for almost five hours now, and I haven't heard one single presenter offer any useful new information or viable solutions.

If this really is a confab of the finest minds in their fields...we're screwed.

A team from Senegal, for example, discussed the inconclusive results of some recent biopsies of the brain tissue of rabid elephants. A Brazilian electrical engineer spoke of her lab's failed attempt to use gamma radiation waves to block the effects of cellphone signals on animal pheromone reception.

A group of officers from Moscow's Valerian Kuybyshev Military Engineering Academy outlined a Kremlin-backed plan to carpet-bomb any and all major underground animal breeding areas. When I angrily interrupted to explain that the American government had tried an almost identical bombing campaign just a few months ago and that it had failed spectacularly, the committee chairman cut the feed to my microphone.

Thank goodness it was time for a fifteen-minute break.

Right now I'm standing in the hallway outside the main meeting room, mainlining some desperately needed caffeine and sugar: a muddy cup of coffee and a rich, gooey Cadbury chocolate-caramel bar.

Sarah is reviewing her notes for a presentation she's giving later about what she's dubbed HMC—Human *Microbial* Conflict— which she believes, based on her research, will be the next, even more terrifying stage in all this madness.

Freitas, meanwhile, is sitting on the floor, talking animatedly on his smartphone and tapping wildly on his iPad. I don't have the foggiest idea to whom or what about—but by the look of it, it's important.

"Feeling nervous?" I ask Sarah when I see she's reached the end of her pages.

"Of course," she replies. "*Exceedingly* nervous."

"Don't worry about it, you'll do great. Just try to imagine that every chubby, balding, pasty scientist in the audience is wearing nothing but his underwear. Actually…no, don't do that. That's a pretty disturbing picture."

Sarah smiles and shakes her head.

"Thanks, Oz. But I'm not nervous about giving the presentation. I'm terrified…about what my *data* show. If you think wild *animals* attacking humans is bad, just wait another few months or so, when I predict wild *bacteria* will join in. There's no way to bomb something microscopic."

"Good God," I mumble, rubbing my temples. The prospect of that sounds beyond horrific. "One crisis at a time, please."

Suddenly Freitas leaps up from the ground and hurries over to us, waving his iPad in the air. Given the glint in his eye, I can tell he's overjoyed about something.

"They're in! The latest worldwide AAPC numbers!"

"Isn't that just a bunch of old fogeys?" I ask.

Freitas doesn't like my joke. The acronym, he says, stands for animal attacks per capita. It's a metric he invented to measure the rate of animal-related incidents and deaths in different countries around the world.

"Over the past few weeks," he explains, "rumors have been flying that all nations are *not* created equal. At least not when it comes to HAC. Allegedly, some have begun seeing a marked decline in attacks, while others have experienced a skyrocketing.

"So," he continues, "I ordered a team of DOE statisticians to crunch all the millions of data points we had and turn them into an easy-to-digest format."

He hands me his iPad. On it is a map of the world shaded every color of the rainbow.

"Uh, okay," I reply skeptically, skimming it. "So it looks like…Finland, Japan, South Korea, and Egypt are seeing fewer attacks. But Brazil, Indonesia, and Canada are seeing more. Big deal. Where does this get us? It doesn't tell us why—or what any of these countries have in common."

"No, it sure doesn't," Freitas responds. "Which is exactly what I want us to find out. Now come on!"

He turns and starts jogging down the hallway—away from the conference room.

"Dr. Freitas!" Sarah calls out, confused. "Where are you going? Our break's almost over. I have a paper to present!"

But Freitas doesn't slow. Instead he glances back and calls out, "Forget your stupid presentation, this is way bigger! We've got a plane waiting to take us to Bali!"

Bali? Is he serious? According to his own data, Indonesia has seen a massive spike in animal attacks recently—and *that's* where he wants to take us?

But when I glance down back at the map on the iPad still in my hands, I see that in the past month, the island of Bali has actually had almost *zero* reported attacks.

That has to be some kind of mistake. Doesn't it?

Or could the key to solving HAC really be right under our nose?

I grab Sarah's arm and practically drag her down the hallway after Freitas.

The day just got a hell of a lot more interesting.

CHAPTER 8

CHLOE IS IN HER old childhood bedroom, lying in her old childhood bed. Eli is curled up in the crook of her arm. The little boy is dozing soundly. Obliviously.

But for Chloe, try as she might, sleep just won't come.

She's been living in her parents' fortified apartment complex for only a few days now, but already she's started losing her mind.

Maybe it's because the air inside is so oppressive and stale: to prevent wild animals from entering, each and every window, chimney, and vent has been double-locked, triple-sealed, and completely boarded up.

Maybe it's because her elderly parents' health has started to deteriorate so rapidly and unexpectedly. Since the last time she saw them, her mother has grown increasingly forgetful, and her father's mobility has become severely limited.

Maybe it's because the apartment's food and supplies are stretched so thin. The government's biweekly rations delivery is inexplicably two days late, so the family is down to their last can of beans, a few shriveled tomatoes from their indoor hydroponic garden, and half of a stale, moldy baguette.

Or, maybe it's because the sounds echoing across the city each night are so utterly terrifying. Screeching cats. Growling dogs. Yowling foxes. Shrieking vultures.

Screaming humans.

As Chloe snuggles Eli a bit closer, her mind drifts to Oz. She's still mad at him for tricking her into staying with her parents in Paris. But of course she understands. He did it out of love. Frankly, had she been in his shoes, their roles reversed, she'd probably have done the same.

Now she just prays that he's safe. They spoke briefly earlier today; he'd called from a plane, somewhere over the Pacific. Something about going to Mali. Africa? No, that wouldn't make sense. But the connection was lost before she could ask more.

Chloe feels her eyelids finally getting heavy. She's just about to doze off when a pounding on the front door practically shakes the apartment's walls.

Eli jolts awake and begins to cry with fright. As Chloe comforts him, she looks over at the clock on her nightstand: 3:18 a.m. Who could it possibly be at this hour?

No one good, Chloe thinks to herself.

She reassures her son she'll be right back and slips out of bed to investigate.

The pounding continues as she passes through the kitchen—and grabs a glistening chef's knife, just in case. Marielle has been woken up, too, but Chloe gestures for her stepmother to stay back and let her handle this.

"*Monsieur Tousignant!* It is the gendarmerie, with rations. Open the door!"

Chloe looks through the peephole. She sees two soldiers standing outside in the eerily dim hallway. One is carrying an assault rifle, the other a cardboard box. Both wear black fatigues and body armor.

Chloe exhales with relief. She sets down the knife, unlocks the deadbolt, and opens the door.

"Bonsoir," she says. "Thank you very much for finally coming. I can take them."

She reaches for the box of food, but the soldier pulls it away.

"I am sorry, *mademoiselle*. This is to be delivered to Jean-Luc Tousignant only."

"It's fine. I'm Chloe Tousignant, his daughter." She glances up and down the hallway, making sure the coast is clear. "Now please give me the rations and shut the door, before an animal manages to—"

"You could be Marie Antoinette, for all I care," the other soldier snarls. "It does not matter." He holds up his smartphone, which is connected to a tiny digital fingerprint scanner. "The thumbprint of each recipient is required for delivery verification."

Chloe can't believe this. "He's in bed. He's sick. The man can barely walk! And I have a four-year-old son who's very hungry. Please."

The first soldier gives her a sympathetic look, but he won't back down.

"The rules are the rules. I am sorry. If you want the rations, your father must accept them personally. If not, we have many more deliveries to make tonight."

Chloe groans in annoyance. French citizens are dying in the streets, they're starving in their homes, and the army is worried about sticking to protocol?

"*Merde!* Fine! Wait here while I—"

Chloe suddenly sees two beady little eyes appear on the hallway ceiling.

In an instant, a furry four-legged animal squeals and leaps down at her.

She bats it away—a giant raccoon just inches from her face. "*Non!*" she yells as it lands on its back on the floor, then quickly rights itself and comes at her again.

Chloe screams and struggles to fight it off as it scrambles up her legs and torso toward her head, its claws digging into her flesh every inch of the way.

The soldier holding the box of rations drops it and frantically comes to Chloe's aid. He rips the rabid animal off her and flings it into the apartment. His partner swiftly aims his rifle and sprays a flurry of gunshots, killing the creature instantly.

Chloe is out of breath. In total shock. Her legs and chest are criss-crossed with bloody scratches. She's otherwise unharmed, but scared. And furious.

"*Merci,*" she snaps at the soldiers—as she scoops up the box of rations they dropped and slams the door in their face, before either has a chance to protest.

Chloe locks the door and grips the box tightly. Marielle, who witnessed the entire episode, is too stunned to say a word. All she and her stepdaughter can do is stare at the raccoon's bloody carcass, and the trail of bullet holes along the floor and wall.

And be thankful that Chloe is still alive.

CHAPTER 9

THIS MUST BE WHAT heaven looks like.

A pristine coastline, dotted with swaying palm trees, stretching as far as the eye can see. White sand, finer than baby powder. Blue water, clear as glass. The sun warm, the breeze cool.

But best of all?

We've been standing out in the open for nearly fifteen minutes now, less than half a mile from thousands of acres of lush tropical forest, brimming with wildlife…

And there hasn't been a single animal attack yet.

I have to admit, it's more than a little eerie. But it's also an incredible relief, a feeling I can barely describe. A definite cause for hope.

"Careful with that," Freitas says to one of the porters. They're unloading our crates of scientific gear off the hotel shuttle from Ngurah Rai International Airport. Along with Freitas, Sarah, and I, sorting the equipment to be brought to our rooms, are Dr. Ti-Hua Chang, an epidemiologist from the Chinese Ministry of Health; Dr. Woodruff, an immunologist from the University of Illinois; and a few other scientists I've exchanged only a handshake with.

Actually, "rooms" is an understatement. They're more like personal luxury villas, designed in the style of traditional Balinese wooden huts. Built on stilts, they're perched directly above the sparkling water. Absolutely gorgeous.

Which could describe the entire hotel. Definitely not the kind of lodging that stingy old Uncle Sam would normally spring for. But thanks to the worldwide economic slump and the island's drastic drop in tourism, Freitas was able to score these stunning accommodations for his team for pennies on the dollar.

They're also in a prime location, on the beach and also near the jungles where we'll be doing the bulk of our testing. Our goal is simple: figure out why animals are running amok around the rest of the world but here in Bali are living with humans in harmony.

I take a quick break and shake out the front of my t-shirt. It's already damp with sweat and clinging to my chest. Not that I'm complaining or anything, but after all those months in the frigid Arctic, I can't remember the last time I was this hot and sticky.

Feeling thirsty, I look around for something to drink. There's a tiki bar on the other end of the open-air hotel lobby, but it looks empty and closed. Maybe there's a water fountain nearby. Or, heck—the sea looks so clear, maybe I'll just drink that.

"Indonesian iced tea, sir?"

A trim young Balinese man in a crisp white uniform is suddenly by my side. He's holding a silver platter on which sits a tall glass of amber liquid with a twist of lemon.

I don't think I've ever seen a more tempting beverage in all my life.

"Wow, yes, thank you. You guys are mind readers!"

I gulp down the sweet, refreshing tea so fast, rivulets of it trickle down my chin.

"Not mind readers, sir. We are simply very good at treating our guests well. And so is our wildlife, as you can see."

I wipe my mouth with the back of my hand, my top lip cold against my warm skin.

"I sure can," I say, intrigued by the hotel attendant's words. Perhaps he knows something that will point us in the right direction. "Any idea why that might be?"

The man thinks for a moment, furrowing his brow.

"Well, most Balinese are Hindu. And most Hindus are vegetarian. We believe in practicing nonviolence against all life forms. Perhaps our animals feel the same way."

I stifle a laugh—at least I try to—which I hope doesn't offend this friendly hotel employee bearing the divine iced tea. He can't be serious, can he? I'm no world religion scholar, but I'm pretty sure there are plenty of Hindus and vegetarians alike in places like India, Pakistan, Nepal, Malaysia. And those countries are reeling from some of the worst animal attacks on the planet.

"Interesting theory" is all I say, placing the empty glass back on the tray and extending my other hand to shake. "I'm Oz, by the way. Thanks again."

"My name is Putu. Welcome to Bali. I hope you find what you are looking for."

That makes two of us.

The porters are wheeling the last of our gear to our villas. I know Freitas will want us to head out as soon as possible to begin running tests. So first, I take out my new international satellite phone, issued to all team members so we can stay in constant touch no matter where in the world we go. Thrilled to see I have a few bars of reception, I scroll down my very short list of contacts until I find the one I so desperately want to call: "Chloe ~ Paris."

"Did he tell you what time the bar opens?"

I look up. Sarah has walked over to me. She's carrying an industrial metal laptop case and wheeling a crate of empty test tubes and plastic specimen bags.

She's also stripped down to cargo shorts and a tight gray tank top. Like me, her skin is glistening with sweat. But unlike me, on her it actually looks pretty sexy.

"Sorry. I didn't ask. And with so few guests, I bet they don't even open it at all."

"Too bad," Sarah replies. "I was thinking, after we spend the day trekking around the island, we could…have a drink. Compare notes."

Huh? I don't believe it. Is star CDC biologist Dr. Sarah Lipchitz…hitting on me?

I can't tell if that glint in her eye is professional curiosity or something more. Sure, it's a scary time to be single and alone in the world. But Sarah knows I'm happily married. This is a path I definitely don't want to go down—especially with a woman as smart and dangerously cute as she is. Maybe I'm reading too much into it.

"Maybe, uh…another time." Then I hold up my satellite phone. "Excuse me."

I step into a quiet corner of the lobby and dial. It rings. And rings. Finally, I hear a click. The sound of rustling. Then a familiar voice. *"Allô?"*

"Chloe? It's Oz! Can you hear me? How are you and Eli doing?"

The connection is awful, full of crackling static. I can barely make out what my wife replies.

"We're fine but…and food is low…and animals keep trying to… please hurry…"

"Chloe, honey," I interrupt, "I can't understand what you're saying. I'm going to hang up. Give Eli a hug for me. I love you both. And…I will hurry. I promise."

I wait for her to answer, but all I hear is more white noise. Then the line goes dead. Which gives me a sudden sinking feeling deep in the pit of my stomach.

My wife and child are under siege in Paris and I'm here in paradise.

I'd better get to work.

CHAPTER 10

MOST MORNINGS, I LIKE to start the day with a shower. Today I feel like taking a dip in the sea, right outside my front door.

I'm standing by the entrance of my wooden villa, gazing out at the crystal water all around me. The sun is just starting to rise, casting vibrant streaks of pink and orange along the horizon.

It's a precious moment of peace before what I know will be another grueling day.

After arriving in Bali yesterday afternoon, our team wasted no time getting down to business. Freitas, Sarah, the other scientists, and I spread out to cover as much ground as we could. We took samples of the water, soil, pollen, and air. We tested the island for unusual patterns of radiation and electromagnetic activity. We dug through mud as thick as tar to collect insects and worms. We waded into a rushing river to net fish and plankton. We even trekked through the punishing jungle in Padangtegal to trap a feisty twenty-two-inch-long macaque. Before we left, Sarah told me to bag a stinking pile of the monkey's dung. I thought she was kidding—or maybe stung by my rejection earlier—but Freitas insisted I obey.

By the time we all made it back to the hotel, well after midnight,

I could barely keep my eyes open. I knew the next day would be even more exhausting: the plan was to head further inland into the mountains to capture additional animals to study, including a Komodo dragon and a six-foot Burmese python. I flopped onto the bed the moment I walked in, still wearing my filthy clothes, and fell fast asleep.

But now, thanks to a mix of jet lag and nerves, I'm wide awake at dawn. It's almost 11:00 p.m. in Paris, too late to call Chloe. To clear my head, I decide to take a dip.

I strip down to my boxers and cannonball into the calm sea, as if I were a little kid again at the local pool. I'm surprised by how warm the water feels, like a soothing bath.

I flick my wet hair from my eyes and float on my back at first, letting the gentle current carry me. Then I flip over and use a slow breaststroke to swim farther out.

I glance over my shoulder at the coastline. The swaying palm trees, the quaint villas, the stunning beach—it's like something you'd see on a postcard. I make a mental note to bring Chloe and Eli back here someday, when all this HAC craziness is finally over, for a family vacation. Lord knows they deserve it.

I know I should probably start heading back to my hut, but something beckons me to swim a little farther out.

Big mistake.

Just up ahead, maybe twenty yards in front of me, I spot a rippling, pinkish-purple mass of something underwater heading my way—fast. Thanks to the way the light is being refracted, I can't quite make out what it is. But I have a very bad feeling.

My first instinct says it's a school of angry jellyfish. Toxic ones.

As the giant blob keeps coming toward me, I realize yes, it *is* a school of jellyfish…with some venomous sea snakes mixed in and a few tiger sharks behind it.

Oh, shit!

"Help, help!" I shout as I twist around and start swimming frantically back toward the shore. "Sarah! Dr. Freitas!"

I'm flapping my arms and kicking my legs wildly, as fast as I can move them. I think I might be getting away, but when I steal a glance behind me, the jellyfish, sea snakes, and tiger sharks are even closer.

I thought Bali was supposed to be safe! What the hell is going on?

I keep swimming and screaming, but it's no use. I can feel the water churning behind me as the mad sea creatures close in. And I can see out of the corner of my eye that they've even started to spread out in a semicircle, flanking me on both sides.

My heart is pounding. My mind is racing.

Is this really how I'm going to die?

Then, in the distance, I hear a glorious sound: the low rumble of a ship engine speeding in my direction. As it gets closer, I hear voices, too, calling to me in Balinese.

Thank God, I think—I hope they're not too late.

I feel a stinger pierce my right ankle and a set of fangs chomp down on my left calf. I howl in pain and try desperately to shake the creatures off…as another jellyfish latches onto my shoulder and a second sea snake latches onto my hip.

I writhe and splash, pain coursing through my body, praying the boat gets here fast. The tiger sharks must be mere yards away, circling, preparing to finish me off.

Finally I spot the noisy vessel. It's a local fishing trawler manned by a group of shirtless Balinese men. Three of them dive into the water and paddle over to me...

And as if by magic, the jellyfish, sea snakes, and tiger sharks all swim away.

I'm too stunned and light-headed to make sense of this. But, Jesus, am I thankful.

The fishermen pull me over to their boat and gently lift me aboard. I'm shocked by all the blood I see. Not mine—the *gallons* of it staining the deck.

While I start to triage my throbbing wounds, I can't help but notice the awful conditions of the sea life on board. Filthy tanks full of bloody fish, crammed together like sardines. Blue crabs stuffed into rusty cages, their shells crushed and mutilated. Even an adorable baby dolphin, tangled in a net, struggling to take its last breaths.

I'm beyond grateful to be alive, but appalled by the horror I'm seeing.

And confused by it, too.

Putu, the hotel attendant I met yesterday—he said most Balinese were Hindu vegetarians who revered all animal life. Clearly that isn't exactly true. Judging by the scene on this boat, fish have plenty to fear from Bali's fishermen. That army of sea creatures fled when the fishermen showed up, but they sure as hell had no problem trying to kill *me*. Why?

My head spins. Maybe animals can distinguish among the human race by scent—whether Hindu vegetarians or dangerous predators—and react accordingly.

For now, as I try to catch my breath and tend to my painful snakebites and jellyfish stings, there's only one thing I know for sure.

Bali isn't the HAC-free paradise we thought it was.

CHAPTER 11

"IT WAS NOT ANOTHER of the dreams in which he had often come back; he was really here. And yet his wife trembled, and a vague but heavy fear was upon her."

Chloe stops reading aloud from *A Tale of Two Cities* and places the well-worn paperback down on her lap, suddenly overcome by emotion.

Charles Dickens wrote those words—about one of the novel's main characters, worried about her husband's safety—in 1859. Yet tonight, for Chloe, they hit painfully close to home. Her mind drifts to Oz, halfway around the world. A "vague but heavy fear" is definitely what she's feeling.

"Mommy, keep reading," says Eli. He's nestled in bed beside her under the covers. It's one of the novels that she and Oz have been reading to Eli, a few pages a night, ever since they were in the Arctic. "Why did you stop?"

"Just lie there, honey. Something tells me you'll fall asleep pretty soon."

Chloe sets down the book, walks to the door, and is about to turn off the light…

When she hears a loud scratching noise coming from outside.

She's used to the occasional sounds of wild animals trying to find their way in, but tonight it's alarmingly loud.

She nervously peels back the bedroom window curtains—and gasps.

Through a crack in the boards between the glass and wrought iron grate she glimpses at least five or six furry, reddish-brown creatures scurrying up the side of the building, tongues dangling out of their mouths, fangs glistening in the moonlight.

She tries to stay calm. She reminds herself how safe she and her family are—relatively speaking—inside this modest Paris apartment, the one in which she grew up. Every door and window has been heavily reinforced and is kept locked practically around the clock. Beyond the fact that all possible entry points had been sealed up, just a few nights ago, after stomping to death a dazed rabid mouse that had managed to crawl in through the shower drain, Chloe even plugged up much of the apartment's plumbing, too.

Still, the sight of this pack of feral animals—dogs? wolves?—scrabbling up the side of her building fills her with quiet dread.

For good measure, Chloe checks the screws securing the iron grate over the window, making sure they're nice and tight. Satisfied, she smooths out the curtain.

"*Bonne nuit,* Eli," she says to her son. "Good night, my love."

He responds with a gentle snore. The boy is fast asleep.

Chloe tiptoes back to the bedroom door, which is suddenly pushed open from the other side. Marielle, her stepmother, is standing at the threshold.

"*Maman?* What is it?"

At first Marielle doesn't speak. She simply blinks, clearly confused.

"I…I'm sorry. I was looking for the bathroom."

Chloe sighs. Looking for the bathroom? She's lived in this apartment for forty years. Clearly her forgetfulness is getting worse. Chloe has suggested they see a doctor, but Marielle has refused. Not that they could get an appointment even if they wanted to. Practically every hospital in the city is strained to capacity treating victims of animal attacks. An old lady with early-stage dementia isn't exactly a top priority.

"It's all right," Chloe says soothingly. "This is Eli's room. My old room, when I was a little girl. Remember? The bathroom is that way. Second door on the left."

"Of course it is," Marielle says, waving her stepdaughter off with a mixture of frustration and embarrassment. But then she adds, with a bashful smile, "And I only had to open every *other* door to find it."

Marielle pads back down the hall. Chloe gives Eli, dozing soundly, a final look. *He deserves a better world than this,* she thinks, turning off the light.

Headed to the kitchen, Chloe suddenly hears vicious growls and violent scratching coming from the other end of the apartment—along with her mother's bloodcurdling screams.

"No, no!" Marielle is shouting. "Chloe, Jean-Luc, help!"

"Maman!" Chloe yells back, rushing to find her.

On her way down the hall, she notices that the guest room door is wide open…the pantry door is wide open…and to her horror, *the front door is wide open, too.*

Chloe understands immediately what's happened. In her stepmother's absentminded search for the bathroom, she has done the unthinkable.

She's just let in the animals.

CHAPTER 12

"MAMAN!" **CHLOE SHOUTS AGAIN,** rummaging frantically around the kitchen for anything she can use to fight back. "I'm coming!"

She uses one hand to grab the first blade she spots, a small paring knife, and the other hand to heave an old frying pan off the stove.

Not the ideal set of weapons, by any means, but they'll have to do.

Chloe rushes toward the gruesome sounds of the struggle emanating from inside the apartment's tiny bathroom. She charges in, desperate to save Marielle's life.

But she isn't at all prepared for the horrifying sight that awaits her.

A pack of feral foxes—the animals Chloe saw earlier climbing up the outside of the building—is literally tearing her elderly stepmother limb from limb.

They're attacking Marielle ravenously, ripping her bloody nightgown to shreds, wrenching whole chunks of flesh from her body as she cries and struggles and screams.

Chloe roars with anger and snaps into action.

She clobbers the nearest fox square on the head with the heavy pan, feeling his skull crunch inward from the impact like a hardboiled egg. She hits another fox, then sinks the paring knife into the furry back of a third.

A fourth fox, realizing Chloe is both a threat and a meal, turns on her, leaping up and clamping his jagged teeth into her thigh.

Chloe yelps in pain but manages to pierce her knife straight into the animal's eyeball, lodging it deep in the socket, before forcefully prying the creature off.

She pummels the animal with the pan, again and again, until finally it dies.

"*Maman!*" she yells, kneeling beside her horrendously disfigured stepmother, nearly slipping on the blood-soaked tile floor.

Marielle is mercifully slipping into unconsciousness. She reaches a trembling hand toward her stepdaughter's face and whispers, in a haze, "Chloe…*ma petite fille*…my sweet girl…"

Then her hand falls to her side. Her last breath escapes her lungs.

Chloe is too shocked to cry. Too staggered to make any sound at all.

But with so much adrenaline still pulsing through her veins, she is *not* too stunned to take action.

"Eli! *Papa!*" she screams, rushing out of the bathroom into the hallway.

She finds her father standing there in his underwear, shaking like a leaf.

"Your stepmother…I heard such terrible noises. Is she…?"

"Yes, Papa. She's—she is dead." Jean-Luc takes a step toward the bathroom to look for himself, but Chloe stops him. "Don't."

Jean-Luc looks past Chloe, into the front hallway, and his eyes grow wide.

Chloe turns around—and sees three pit bulls trotting into the apartment through the still-open front door.

"Come on, we have to hurry!" Chloe implores, trying to pull her father along.

But with surprising strength, Jean-Luc resists. He grips his daughter's shoulder tightly and looks her straight in the eye.

"*Non,* Chloe. I am a slow, old man. It is my time. You and Eli—*you* must go."

Chloe is left aghast by her father's command, and by the ultimate sacrifice he is insisting he make for his daughter and grandson. She wants to argue with him, *plead* with him, to reconsider, but she knows his mind is made up.

"I love you," is all she says, then turns and dashes back to Eli's room.

She makes it inside and slams the door shut behind her—just moments before she hears this second wave of animals begin brutally mauling her frail father.

She finds Eli awake in bed, cowering under the blankets, crying. Chloe rushes over and sweeps him into her arms.

"Eli, it's okay, sweetie, Mommy's here. We have to go!"

But how? Not through the front door: the apartment is now crawling with wild animals. But not through the window, either: even if she could break the boards, that metal grate is bolted on tight.

Are they trapped?

No. Chloe gets an idea.

She flings open the closet and pushes aside some of her old childhood clothes that are still hanging there, revealing a small trapdoor: a dumbwaiter, dating back to the turn of the century, when the apartment building was one single luxury home and Chloe's bedroom was part of the servant's quarters. She discovered this odd historical remnant as a girl and treated it as a secret cubby, a hiding spot for dolls and diaries.

Now, as she pries off the wooden plank she nailed over it only a few days earlier, she hopes it just might save their lives.

She opens the squeaky door and orders Eli to wiggle inside first. "I know you're scared," she says. "I am, too. But I'll be right behind you. You can do it!"

The boy bravely obeys. Chloe squeezes in after him and the two carefully climb down this dark, dusty chamber, using ledges and splintery boards.

They finally make it to the ground floor—a former kitchen converted long ago into a garage. Chloe kicks open the trapdoor and she and Eli crawl out.

The space is cluttered and dark, and Chloe can't find the light switch. Taking Eli's hand, she gropes her way to the manual sliding garage door. She strains to pull it open a few feet, and together mother and son slip out onto the sidewalk—the first time either has stepped foot outside the apartment building in almost two weeks.

Chloe's heart is thumping wildly as she scans the eerily abandoned, trash-strewn Paris streets. The occasional animal growl or human scream echoes in the distance.

Now what?

Her parents are both dead. Their apartment, her only refuge, is overrun with feral animals. Her husband is God knows where, returning God knows when. Her son is cold, tired, terrified. And so is she.

Choking back tears, Chloe scoops Eli into her arms and does the only thing she can think of.

She runs.

CHAPTER 13

"IT DOESN'T MAKE ANY damn sense!" Freitas exclaims, hurling a giant binder full of molecular charts and data graphs clean across our plane's cabin.

He's steaming mad, but Sarah and the other scientists and I are so exhausted we barely react. It feels like we've been discussing our recent findings and debating our hypotheses—make that our *lack* of recent findings and our *flawed* hypotheses—since the moment we left Bali. Hours ago.

We're not far from our next destination. But we're still light-years away from any kind of solution to the animal crisis.

"We should have stayed in Bali longer," Sarah says, "like I wanted to. Those jungles, that sea—they're home to thousands of different species. We ran experiments on less than one percent of them."

"That's still dozens of different animals," I say. "Not all of which, let me remind you"—I hold up my arms, showing some painful jellyfish stings and bandaged sea snake bites—"were as 'friendly' as we were led to believe."

Indeed, my own unfortunate episode in the water turned out to be just the beginning. Over the next few days, two other groups from our

team fended off sudden animal attacks. First a swarm of so-called glid-
ing lizards. Then a stampede of banteng, a breed of wild cattle. Can't
say I'm sorry I missed it.

"We sequenced their DNA," I continue. "We ran brain scans. Conducted autopsies. If I remember correctly," I add sarcastically, "*somebody* even collected and ran tests on monkey droppings. And we
found *nothing* out of the ordinary. No unusual radiation or electromagnetic patterns, either. No strange chemicals in the water or magic
fairy dust in the air. Nil. *Nada.* We spent ninety-six hours in Bali and
all I got was this lousy t-shirt. And, oh, yeah—I almost lost my life."

The other government scientists on board all mumble in agree-
ment. Sarah folds her arms. She won't concede anything to me—I
think out of spite. But she doesn't *disagree* with me, either. Which I
guess I'll take as a sign of progress?

Freitas checks his watch and pensively rubs his beard. I've known
the guy less than two weeks, but I'd swear there's more gray hair in it
now than when I met him.

Sensing a lull in our endless discussion, I take out my international
satellite phone and dial Chloe again in Paris. One of the perks of traveling on a government plane is that you get to use your government
cellphone during the flight.

Not that it does me any good at the moment.

I've been calling the Tousignant apartment hourly since we took
off, but no one's answering. Which happens again this time. The land-
line rings and rings, and then the answering machine kicks in. I've
already left a few increasingly nervous messages, so I hang up. Just for
the heck of it, I dial Chloe's old American cellphone number, which

we shut off after moving to the Arctic. I'm not surprised when I get an automated message telling me the number's no longer in service, but it still feels a little ominous.

I close my eyes for a moment, desperate to calm my nerves and push the creeping fear I'm feeling out of my mind. There must be a simple explanation, right? Maybe the neighborhood's phone lines are down. Maybe the power's out. Maybe Chloe and her family left for an even safer location. Or maybe…maybe…

I guess I dozed off there for a little while, because when I open my eyes again I see Freitas, Sarah, and the others all buckling their seat belts for landing.

I look out my window. We're coming up fast on our destination: Johannesburg. A sprawling metropolis flanked by an enormous nature preserve to the south and teeming slums to the west.

We've come here, Freitas explained before takeoff, because unlike Bali, it's a major urban area facing a markedly *high* rate of animal attacks, and he wants us to conduct a series of parallel tests and experiments for comparison.

But I'm not sure I buy that. In fact, I think there's something he's not telling us.

Jakarta, Bangkok, Manila, Sydney—these are all big cities that *also* have high rates of animal attacks, and each is a much shorter trip from Bali than Johannesburg is. Flying all the way across the Indian Ocean to South Africa took us nearly fifteen hours. Freitas knows one of the most precious resources we have in our hunt for a solution to HAC is time. He wouldn't waste it without a very good reason.

Still peering out my window, I think I've just spotted it.

A massive, swirling flock of birds—they look like white-backed vultures, or maybe falcons—seems to be heading right for us like an airborne tornado.

Some of the other scientists notice it, too, and like me are gripping their armrests, bracing for an attack…

That never comes. Instead, as the birds pass close by our plane, I realize a few of them don't look like any I've ever seen before—except maybe in *Jurassic Park*.

Did I just glimpse some scales? Beaks lined with sharp teeth? Reptilian heads?

If I didn't know better, I'd say some of them looked positively… *prehistoric*.

CHAPTER 14

I'M HANGING ON WITH all my might as our convoy of SUVs weaves along this rough, badly potholed road. Our vehicle is topping forty, maybe fifty miles per hour, tossing us around inside like ice cubes in a cocktail shaker.

But I don't want to slow down one bit. In fact, I wish we'd speed up.

We're cruising along Bertha Street, a major downtown Johannesburg thoroughfare, and the chaos outside is some of the most appalling I've seen.

Gray-furred vervet monkeys are swinging from power lines, hooting and screeching. Leopards are leaping from abandoned car to abandoned car. A flock of goshawks is circling and cawing overhead. Giant baboons are scaling darkened skyscrapers. Military Humvees are overturned, hastily built barricades sit abandoned. Bloody, rotting human carcasses litter the streets. The few living souls I spot are crouched on terraces and rooftops, firing off high-powered rifles at any and all creatures they can—the final holdouts, desperately defending their homes, refusing to surrender.

The entire city center of Johannesburg has been overrun by

wildlife. The phrase "concrete jungle" suddenly has a whole new meaning. I'm speechless.

Freitas is sitting in the front seat. "This place," he says with a wry smirk, "is a little different from Bali, wouldn't you agree?"

As if on cue, a vervet monkey drops down onto our windshield and starts frantically scratching at the glass.

Sarah recoils, but I'm transfixed. For a brief moment, I see a slight resemblance in him to Attila, a lovable chimpanzee I rescued from a medical testing lab years ago and kept as a pet when I lived in New York City. I cared for that little guy deeply...until he turned to the animal dark side, like all the rest.

"Get off of there, you damn stupid ape!" barks Kabelo, our local driver and guide. I can't help but snicker at what I assume is an accidental similarity to Charlton Heston's famous line in *Planet of the Apes*. Kabelo turns the windshield wipers on high and swerves back and forth a few times until the primate is thrown from the car.

"Yeah," I respond now to Freitas. "Ain't exactly another tropical paradise, that's for sure."

Sarah, sitting next to me, folds her arms. "I don't know how in the world you expect us to collect any specimens here," she says, an unusual level of agitation in her voice.

Not that I blame her. If this is what the city core looks like, I don't want to imagine what's happening in the nature preserve on the outskirts, which is where we're headed.

"The doctor makes a good point," I say. "There are just too many animals running around. Trying to capture and autopsy even one of them—that's suicide."

"Kabelo, be careful!" Freitas shouts as our SUV narrowly avoids getting T-boned by a charging stampede of big-horned Cape buffalo.

Our fearless leader takes a deep breath, then turns around to face Sarah and me and the other scientists in our vehicle. I can tell there's something on his mind, something he's debating whether or not to share.

"You're right. Trying to trap one of these animals? That *is* suicide. Thankfully, that's not why we've come to South Africa."

My told-you-so internal celebration is brief. I start to get nervous. Why *are* we here?

"There have been rumors," Freitas continues, "that the…'affliction'…has started spreading. To *humans*."

Huh? I glance around the vehicle at Sarah and the others. This is clearly the first time any of *us* are hearing that rumor.

"There have been unconfirmed sightings," Freitas says, "matching similar classified reports from elsewhere around the world—which I've convinced Washington to suppress—of a group of rabid individuals living in the Suikerbosrand Nature Reserve. Locals now consider *them* to be the most dangerous creatures in the area."

Freitas pauses solemnly. Then adds: "We're here to capture one. And prevent this global epidemic from entering an even more devastating phase."

My jaw is literally hanging open. Sarah and the others are stammering.

What the hell is this guy talking about?

For the past umpteen years, the planet has been battling HAC, Human-*Animal* Conflict. It's *animals* whose behavior has been going haywire, thanks to the abundance of petroleum-derived hydrocarbons in the environment being chemically altered by cellphone radiation waves. It's *animals* who have been rising up and attacking innocent people because human scents have been chemically altered, too, and are now perceived as attack pheromones. And it's animals—and *only* animals—who are susceptible to this because *Homo sapiens* lacks the highly sensitive vomeronasal organ almost all other creatures possess that detects airborne pheromones in the first place.

This isn't just some personal hunch of mine. It's *the* accepted theory about the animal crisis within the mainstream scientific community—and it has been for quite some time. It's been tested and duplicated in labs around the world.

Now we're talking about Human-*Human* Conflict? No. No way. It's anatomically impossible. Absurd. The fact that we're even chasing after this urban legend at all is a ridiculous waste of time and resources. If it's true, yes, of course, it would upend our entire understanding of what's been going on. But it *can't* be. Right?

"I understand this is a lot to process," Freitas says. "And frankly, I'm praying that the rumors turn out to be false. But you can understand why the government insisted we come and find out for certain. Because if the stories *are* correct, and if it spreads…"

He trails off and shakes his head. The doomsday scenario he's alluding to—millions, maybe billions of *people* suddenly turning on each other like vicious beasts—is too horrifying to even say out loud.

Through my window I see we've reached the outskirts of the city. The buildings are beginning to thin out and the landscape is looking more verdant.

Soon we'll be arriving at the nature preserve, so I take out my satellite phone and try calling Chloe and Eli in Paris one final time.

It's not that I won't have service inside the park. It's that apparently, I'll have my hands full trying to track and tranquilize a goddamn feral human being.

The line rings and rings. I've been calling for hours now and there's still no answer. Even for an optimist like myself, it's getting harder and harder not to worry.

Not just about my family. About the future of the human race.

CHAPTER 15

WE'VE BEEN TREKKING ALONG this jungle trail for less than fifteen minutes and already I'm drenched with sweat.

Kabelo and Dikotsi, and a few other local guides are at the head of our group, hacking away at vines and tree limbs with huge machetes to help clear our path. Still, the underbrush is dense and uneven. We're all lugging heavy gear and carrying firearms. The midday African sun is directly overhead, beating down on us without mercy.

Freitas puts a pair of high-powered binoculars to his eyes, awkwardly shifting the McMillan M1A assault rifle slung over his shoulder. The man may be a brilliant scientist, but he's clearly not very comfortable toting such a bulky weapon.

To be fair, neither am I. Especially since mine has a bayonet.

"Remember," Freitas says, addressing the team. "These are *people* we're after. Not animals. We have no idea how the sickness will have affected them. Whether they'll be savage or intelligent. Whether they'll attack unarmed or with weapons. Whether they—"

"Oh, give it a break, doc!" I exclaim. "I'm sorry, but I just can't listen to this nonsense. We're facing a serious global crisis here, and you're making us hike through a dangerous jungle in search of the living dead? This is nuts!"

"I don't disagree, Oz," Freitas replies. "After the order came in, believe me, I pushed back. But when President Hardinson calls you herself, it's not easy to say no."

Jesus. I've learned by now that Freitas isn't a very good actor. From his expression, I think he's telling the truth. So the *White House* thinks there's a real chance HAC might have spread to humans. Maybe it's not just a dumb rumor after all.

"Fine," I say. "Let's assume these feral humans really do exist. How do we possibly explain it—scientifically? We'd have to throw out the entire pheromone theory."

"Not necessarily," says Sarah. She's blotting her glistening forehead with a bandana. I've forgotten how hot she looks when she's, well…hot.

"*Yes* necessarily," I reply. "HAC is caused by animals misinterpreting human scents as attack pheromones, which triggers aggressive behavior. And they detect those pheromones through the VNO gland at the base of their nasal cavity. A gland that human beings don't possess."

"You're saying humans aren't affected by pheromones at all, Oz? Come on."

"Despite what the makers of Axe body spray might have you believe," I answer, "the scientific jury is still out on that one."

"Precisely," says Freitas. "Perhaps we perceive them in a different way. Perhaps these feral humans aren't using their olfactory organs at all. Maybe they're absorbing pheromones through mucous tissue in their lungs."

"Right, like how nicotine is absorbed from smoking," says Sarah. "Simple."

I exhale a long sigh—and suddenly can't help but wonder what scary, invisible airborne particles might have just entered my bloodstream. I hate to admit it, but Sarah and Freitas have the beginnings of a decent working theory. I just pray it's not needed.

"All right," I concede. "Maybe it's possible. But that still doesn't explain—"

"*Gevaar, gevaar!*" shouts one of our guides, suddenly dropping his machete and whipping out his Desert Eagle handgun. I don't speak Afrikaans, but I understand exactly what he's saying. *Danger.*

Our whole team freezes, and we scramble to ready our weapons.

Something is rushing frantically through the dense bushes to our left. I can't make out what—or *who*—it is, but it's heading right for us, fast.

Kabelo raises his rifle and unleashes a volley of shots in their direction.

"Don't shoot!" Freitas yells, grabbing Kabelo's gun. "We need them alive!"

"I need *me* alive more!" he huffs, shaking off Freitas's grip.

"There may not be many of them," Freitas pleads. "And they are your countrymen. Please, at least hold your fire until we see what they—"

"They're jackals!" I shout, almost relieved to glimpse some furry paws and pointy snouts through the leaves, instead of human hands and heads. "Let's take 'em out!"

I start shooting my Armalite AR-10 first, and the rest of the team quickly follows suit. We're bombarding the underbrush with bullets, but it's impossible to see how many jackals we've hit—or how many in the pack are still charging at us.

The remaining animals—about five or six of them—finally burst out of the vegetation, all yipping and frantically snapping their sharp jaws. They're fast as hell and impossible to hit, even by over a dozen men and women with semiautomatic weapons.

Three jackals get close enough to attack. Dr. Chang gets a big chunk of his leg bitten off by one before stabbing it to death with a bowie knife. A second jackal lunges at Kabelo, who crushes its head with his rifle.

A final jackal leaps up directly at me—but I shoot it, midair, and it's dead before it hits the ground.

We all take a moment to catch our breath and regroup. Chang's injury is much more than a flesh wound, but he'll survive.

I wipe off the jackal blood that splattered onto my face when I shot the animal from such close range. If I'd missed? I wouldn't have much of a face *left*.

Then another thought enters my head. An even grimmer one.

If a pack of three-foot-long rabid jackals almost managed to kill us…just imagine what a pack of feral humans could do.

CHAPTER 16

CHLOE STEPS OUT INTO the wet Paris afternoon, holding Eli in her arms. She had hoped the rain might have let up by now, but the day is getting late and it's still coming down in buckets.

Screw it, Chloe thinks, draping a slimy plastic trash bag over her and her son's heads. She'd rather get a little wet than be out on the street after dark.

And they have a hell of a lot of ground to cover.

It feels like a lifetime ago, but it was only last night that she and Eli barely made it out of her parents' apartment building alive. She'd flagged down a gendarmerie Jeep, but there was little the exhausted soldiers could do to help. They gave her directions to the nearest emergency government shelter, only a few kilometers away, but warned it was already filled to twice its intended capacity.

It wasn't worth the risk. Chloe ducked inside the first suitable place she saw—an abandoned bakery—and hunkered down with Eli for the night.

Using napkins and pastry boxes as tinder, she started a small fire—not just for warmth, but in hopes that the flames would help hide her and her son's scents from any nearby creatures. Chloe also found a few ancient mille-feuille pastries still in the cracked display case, which she shared with Eli as a little treat. They were hard as rocks but, given the circumstances, tasted absolutely *delicious.*

Early the next morning, the rain came. Chloe considered staying inside the bakery, where it was nice and dry, but decided against it.

Oz would likely be calling the apartment to check in, and he would grow sick with worry when no one answered. Chloe knew she had to let her husband know that she and Eli were all right. She'd memorized his satellite phone number, thankfully, but how could she—

No. First things first. Chloe had to get somewhere safe. That was the priority.

But where? She racked her brain. Government shelters were bursting at the seams, and she'd heard horror stories about the conditions inside. She still had a few old friends and distant relatives in the city, but no way of contacting them or even learning if they were alive—let alone if they'd take her and Eli in. She could try to get ahold of Oz, but even if he pulled every string he could at the highest levels of the American government, an evacuation would take too long.

There *was* one other option.

About a week ago, Chloe had overheard her stepmother speaking with a neighbor, a middle-aged political science professor named Pierre. He'd heard from a colleague that a few hundred people had built a shelter, or a fortified commune, at Versailles—not inside the famous palace itself but somewhere close by. It was open to all and apparently safer, cleaner, and better run than any government one.

Chloe has no idea whether this magical place really exists or not. But the Batterie de Bouviers, an old fortification built in the 1870s, is a few miles from the palace gardens and would make the perfect spot for it.

Versailles is over ten miles from the center of Paris, roughly where she is now. That's a grueling hike with a four-year-old on a perfect day. On a cold and rainy one, with feral animals stalking the streets? Forget it.

Chloe knows she might be insane for putting any faith at all into this too-good-to-be-true rumor. But, really, what other choice does she have?

Pulling the trash bag around the two of them like a shawl, Chloe sets out with Eli.

In the waning daylight, she certainly feels safer than she did last night. But she can finally see in full, stark relief just how hellish things have gotten in her beloved city. The shattered storefronts. The overturned cars and buses. The gutters flowing with human blood.

Clutching Eli even closer, she turns onto Boulevard Saint-Michel. Once one of the city's scenic tree-lined streets, it now looks like a deserted war zone.

Chloe is hurrying along the sidewalk, staying close to the buildings for cover…when she hears something. A low rumbling. Or growling. Speeding toward her.

She tenses. She says a silent prayer. She looks up.

But it's not an animal.

It's a gray Citroën Jumper, a boxy commercial van. It screeches to a halt beside her and its rear doors fly open.

"*Mes amis!*" says one of the young women inside, flashing Chloe a clownlike grin and holding what looks like a medieval dagger. "My friends! You must get off the street. It is not safe. Come with us, quickly!"

Like the other seven or eight people crammed inside the van, this woman's head is completely shaved, and she's wearing a flowing brown robe tied at the waist.

Chloe stands completely frozen—terrified, but trying desperately not to look it. She's never seen these freaks before in her life.

But she knows exactly who they are.

"You are…the Fraterre?" she asks nervously.

"*Oui!*" the woman happily exclaims. "Now hurry, we don't have much time!"

The Fraterre, short for La Fraternité de la Terre. The Brotherhood of the Earth.

Chloe has heard rumors about this group, an eccentric cult—part Greenpeace, part Heaven's Gate. It sprung up across France over the past few months in bizarre, quasi-spiritual *solidarité* with Mother Nature. No one knows much about them other than that they're a bunch of nut jobs who think HAC is a divine blessing. They have allegedly assaulted and even killed those who disagree with them.

And now a van full of armed Fraterre cultists are ordering Chloe and Eli to get in.

Chloe stutters. Her mind is racing. What about the fortification near Versailles? What about calling Oz? Then again, maybe this group can actually help keep her safe—at least for the time being?

"*Merci beaucoup,*" she says at last with a big, fake smile.

She climbs inside, Eli in her arms, her heart jackhammering in her chest. The doors are slammed shut and the van peels out.

"Where are we going?"

CHAPTER 17

MY BACK AND KNEES are killing me. Sweat is stinging my eyes. What I wouldn't give right now just to stand up straight for a few seconds and blot my brow.

But I know that would probably be a death wish.

Freitas, Sarah, the other scientists, and I have been crawling through the underbrush on our hands and knees for what feels like ages. We've been moving slowly, deliberately, painstakingly. We've been careful not to make a sound or get too close.

Why?

We've been following a small band of *feral humans*.

Yup. We found the bastards.

And they're freaky beyond belief.

Freitas spotted them first, though he didn't even realize it. After Chang's jackal bite, two of our guides offered to lead the scientist out of the jungle to get first aid. Less than ten minutes later, Freitas noticed a group of people out in front of us. Initially he thought they were members of our team who'd somehow gotten lost. He nearly called out to them—until I literally cupped his mouth with my hand, grabbed his high-powered binoculars, and took a look for myself.

All I managed to croak was, "Mother of God."

I counted five of them. Adults. A mix of men and women, black and white, old and young. They were wearing clothes, normal ones, but dirty and tattered, as if they'd been living in the jungle for weeks. One was carrying a bolt-action rifle, the others a mix of knives, shovels, and other tools. They were walking upright but slightly hunched over, their arms swinging unnaturally, almost gorilla-like.

They looked, in a word, *primal*.

Even from so far away, I could see a scary deadness in their expressions. They were regular humans on the outside. But was there any soul left inside?

Freitas immediately gave the order for all of us to crouch down and follow. We crawled behind them, maybe fifty or sixty yards, tracking as the group lumbered deeper and deeper into the nature preserve.

At one point I asked Freitas in a whisper what our plan was. How much longer would we be stalking these "people"? How would we ever capture one? He admitted he didn't know yet. For now, he just wanted to observe them in their natural habitat.

Yeah, right. What we're looking at? Nothing "natural" about it.

Fine, I thought. Let's see where this goes. Let's see where they lead us. Let's see what they do next.

That was almost half an hour ago. We're still crawling along after them, inching our way through the prickly vegetation. We pass a babbling brook. My hands and face are getting rubbed raw, but I push on....

When suddenly the five feral humans freeze. They prick up their ears. Their senses switch to high alert. They raise their weapons.

I trade nervous glances with Freitas and Sarah. Do they know we're behind them? Have they picked up our scent? Are we in danger?

The "leader" of the pack grunts something, and in a flash the five humans start running—*away* from us, farther into the jungle.

"Go, go!" Freitas commands. "After them!"

Too surprised to argue, we all leap to our feet and pursue. But, damn, are those rabid humans fast! Even our African guides are having trouble keeping up.

At last we reach the crest of a small hill. Gasping for breath, I spot the five humans in the valley below—and I gesture wildly at Freitas, Sarah, and the others to hang back and duck down again.

I've just realized why they've been running.

They're *hunting*.

But not us. Their target is a kudu, a grayish-white antelope they've managed to separate from its herd and surround.

I expect the animal to start attacking the humans any second. But instead, it nervously leaps and prances every which way, looking for an escape. Carefully, the lead human raises his rifle and fires a single shot—striking the antelope's hind leg. The creature falls to the ground, crippled but very much alive.

Now things *really* start to get weird.

The five humans encircle the animal and all place their hands around its neck. Slowly they tighten their grip, choking the helpless antelope as it wheezes and struggles, finally exhaling its last breath.

In unison, the humans bow their heads. They release a low, guttural moan, almost as if in prayer. I'm reminded of the waiter in Bali, who attributed the island's lack of animal attacks to the Hindu respect for all life.

Then they bare their teeth and sink them directly into the antelope's flesh.

They viciously tear through its fur, exposing the crimson muscle tissue and tendons underneath. They rip jagged chunks off with their mouths, like a pride of lions eviscerating a fresh kill. They gulp down the raw meat whole, without chewing. Their mouths and cheeks are covered in blood.

Freitas, Sarah, the scientists, our guides, and I watch this feeding frenzy with a mix of disbelief and revulsion. It's like something straight out of a horror movie, except it's happening maybe three hundred feet in front of us.

"Still want to try to capture one of 'em?" I whisper to Freitas.

He just flashes me a grim look. Of course the answer is yes.

But we both know the task just got a whole lot scarier.

Before long, the antelope carcass has been reduced to virtually a skeleton. The feeding is slowing down in speed and intensity. The meal is almost over.

We're all holding our breath. Waiting to see what these wild humans will do next…

When a digital beeping noise suddenly pierces the jungle air.

Jesus Christ—my satellite phone is ringing!

The humans all turn and look up in our direction. The leader lets out a deep, furious roar.

They've spotted us.

CHAPTER 18

"DON'T SHOOT!" FREITAS DESPERATELY implores, but it's no use. He's lost all control over our group. It's every man for himself.

And it's absolute bedlam.

Many team members have already run off, but a few guides and scared scientists stay behind. They use our elevated position to their advantage and let loose a torrent of gunfire at the feral humans in the valley below as they scatter in all directions.

I watch two of the humans get hit. But the other three don't—and quickly disappear into the dense foliage, dashing back up the hillside in our direction.

"Come on!" I yell to Sarah and Freitas as I turn around to run back the way we came. I see Sarah is on board, but Freitas is pointing somewhere else.

"I think if we cut across the hill, we can probably make it back—"

"Sorry, doc. You're on your own."

I'm already on the run for my life. I'm not about to risk getting lost on top of that.

I start hauling ass back through the jungle. Branches scrape my arms and face as I whip past. All around me I hear gunshots ringing and screams echoing.

Sarah's sprinting just to my left. But after I pass the bubbling creek I remember crawling past minutes earlier, she's suddenly disappeared. I've lost her.

"Sarah?" I call, slowing down the tiniest bit.

She doesn't respond. But I do hear *another* voice.

This one is deep and scratchy. With a South African accent. It comes from close by, but it somehow sounds distant. Haunting.

"We…are…human!"

Holy shit!

I do a quick 360-degree spin, searching for the source. My eyes dart everywhere, but I don't see a soul.

"Hello?" I shout. "Where are you? *Who* are you?"

"Do not…be afraid! We…will not…hurt you. Please, listen… to me!"

I turn now toward the direction of the voice and aim my rifle at it—not easy to do with my adrenaline pumping and my hands trembling.

For the briefest moment, I wonder if maybe this feral human is being honest. The way they ate that antelope was savage, but how they killed it was almost reverent. Maybe they do have respect for human life. Maybe they *aren't* vicious killers like the rest of the animal kingdom. Maybe we pre-judged them too quickly. Maybe—

"Arrrrrgh!"

One of the males lunges out of the tree line and charges at me, baring his teeth and brandishing a pickaxe.

I squeeze the trigger and pepper his chest with rounds. But he keeps coming, swinging his axe wildly.

At the last possible moment I crouch down and spear my bayonet up and into his chest—piercing him clean through the heart.

He releases his axe and flails. He gurgles blood. Finally he goes limp, and I shove him to the jungle floor.

"You…you sneaky son of a bitch!" I shout at his bloody corpse.

I'm livid. I can't believe I doubted for even one millisecond that he wanted to kill me. These savages are *worse* than the animals. They have tools at their disposal. I don't just mean guns and pickaxes. They have language. Cognition. *Trickery*.

I take off running again, equal parts furious and fearful. I yell team members' names—Sarah, Freitas, Kabelo, and some of the others—but I get no response.

I keep moving. I hope I'm still headed in the right direction, but I'm starting to feel light-headed. All the trees and shrubs are starting to look alike.

"Help, help me!" I hear a woman scream, from somewhere not too far away.

That voice is one I instantly recognize: Sarah's.

I switch course and sprint toward it. Not wanting to give up the potential element of surprise, I don't yell back.

And I'm very glad I don't. When I finally see her, she's being chased by a lone female feral human holding a pitchfork—who is quickly gaining.

I raise my rifle but can't get a clean shot, so I loop around to outflank her primal pursuer.

As soon as they reach a clearing, I plow into the woman like a linebacker and tackle her to the ground.

We roll around in the underbrush together, grappling viciously. For such a small woman, she's strong as an ox.

Grunting and straining—employing some of the moves I learned on my JV high school wrestling team—I finally manage to flip her on her back and pin her down.

She starts speaking to me in that same eerie, scratchy voice the man had, in an African language I don't understand. I assume she's begging for her life. Or trying to trick me again somehow. *Not this time.* I swing my rifle around from behind my back and position the bayonet blade inches from her throat…

"Oz, don't!" yells Sarah, rushing over to me. "Remember? We need her alive!"

Damnit. She's right. After all that talk of how we were going to trap a feral human, I've just done it by accident. Still, staring into this woman's beady, almost ghostly eyes, the desire to end her miserable life is overwhelming. But I resist.

"Grab her legs," I order Sarah. "Until we can find the others."

"You mean us?"

I look over to see Dr. Freitas, Kabelo, and many others hurrying toward us.

They practically pile onto the thrashing woman, helping me restrain her. I'm grateful for the assistance—she's incredibly strong.

"Is everyone all right?" I ask Freitas, still trying to catch my breath.

"Dr. Langston…he didn't make it. His death was…ugly. And our guide Dikotsi was mauled pretty badly. Some of the others are tending to him now."

I ease myself off of the feral woman and help flip her onto her stomach, allowing Kabelo to zip-tie her hands. Freitas and the others just stare at her, seemingly numb.

"Very well done, Oz," he says, patting my shoulder. "We've got what we came for. I'll call our pilot and tell him we're ready to fly."

"Really, now," I say skeptically. "And how are you gonna do that?"

Kabelo looks up at me and flashes a crooked grin.

"The white man forgets *again* he is carrying a cellphone?"

Everyone laughs. Including myself. It feels good. A release.

Even the feral woman starts to cackle.

CHAPTER 19

I'M TORN BETWEEN TWO women: the most important one in my life, and quite possibly the most important one in the world.

Getting the captured feral human onto our plane was no easy task. It took five of us—five grown men—just to carry this one petite, flexi-cuffed young woman out of the jungle and back to our waiting vehicles. Unbelievably strong, she kept kicking, thrashing, and trying to bite us the whole time.

She also ranted in her scratchy, eerie voice. One of our guides happened to speak a few words of Tswana, the indigenous language she was using. *"Someone help me!"* he translated. *"I am a person, not a wild animal!"*

Technically, I suppose she was correct. But I've worked on the HAC crisis for many years now and have faced down more deadly predators than I can count. And she is by far the most ferocious and terrifying one I've ever seen.

As we finally got the woman secured into one of our SUVs, Dr. Woodruff said, "I just figured out who this pain in the ass reminds me of." He has a wicked sarcastic streak. "Helen, my ex-wife."

Of course, the name stuck.

Our convoy sped back through the mayhem of Johannesburg to the airport. We buckled "Helen" into a seat in the rearmost row of our Boeing C-40 military transport plane, her arms and legs strapped in as if she were in an electric chair. An emergency oxygen mask around her face kept her from biting or spitting.

We got airborne as quickly as we could, and not just because time was of the essence. We all knew that what we were doing—kidnapping an innocent foreign citizen and transporting her overseas against her will—put us in a legal gray area, to say the least.

We'd been flying for nearly thirty minutes before I remembered—in all the chaos and confusion of the past hour or so, I'd completely forgotten about my satellite phone, and the ring that alerted the pack of feral humans to our presence.

When I finally checked it, I saw I had a new voicemail, from a blocked number.

Hearing Chloe's voice, my relief was indescribable—until I listened through to the end.

Sounding remarkably calm, my wife explained how their apartment had been overrun by animals a few days ago. How she and Eli had managed to escape after her father and stepmother were killed. How they'd spent a night in a shelter from the streets but now were safe.

"We'll be staying with some, uh, *friends* for a while," she said. "Friends of the Earth. I can't tell you where exactly. But I also can't wait to see you, Oz. So you can…*hold me in your arms*. Okay, I love you. Bye."

I knew immediately my wife was in trouble.

One night, years ago, "Hold Me in Your Arms," a painfully cheesy 1988 love song by Rick Astley, came on at a bar where Chloe and I were having one of our first official dates. We joked that being forced to listen to such an awful tune on an endless loop would be even worse than an animal attack. Since then, "hold me in your arms" has become a kind of inside joke between us, a code phrase we use anytime something is bad or corny or scary.

Or, in this case, I could only presume, *dangerous.*

My wife wouldn't say those words unless something wasn't right. I'm certain of it. And those "friends of the Earth" she's staying with— who the hell are they? What is she talking about? Why "can't" she say where she is? What is she scared of?

All I know is, I need to find her and Eli right away and get them out of there fast.

"Freitas!" I shout, marching up the aisle to his seat. "We're changing course!"

"What in God's name are you talking about?" he asks. "We're en route to INL."

That would be the Idaho National Laboratory, the federal government's largest research facility with a dedicated biological sciences unit, nestled in the state's secluded eastern desert. There we'll poke and prod Helen and use every known test in existence on her.

"First we're going back to Paris," I say.

I tell him about the voicemail. What Chloe said. The coded message. My gut instinct that something is very wrong. And that even if *I'm* the one who's wrong, my wife and son are still all alone in a foreign city overrun by wild animals.

"Oz, we can't go there right now. It's too far out of our way. We've got a feral human on board! Don't you understand that? We have to get her to the lab ASAP."

I can't believe what I'm hearing.

"There is no one in the world more committed to solving this crisis than I am," I fire back, my voice rising. Sarah and some of the other scientists are starting to look over at us. "But you're asking me just to forget about my family? Imagine if it was yours!"

Freitas sighs deeply. "I consider the entire *planet* to be my family."

As a fellow man of science, I know what he means. And I respect it.

But as a husband and father, I think it's absolute horseshit.

"You promised me—*promised*—that if I left the Arctic, came along on this wild goose chase of yours, and helped you people stop HAC once and for all, you'd ensure my family's safety. Remember that?" I'm nearly trembling with rage now. "I'm not *asking* you, Dr. Freitas. I am *telling* you. Before Idaho, we are going to France!"

Freitas rubs his salt-and-pepper beard, clearly torn. Maybe I'm getting through to him. Every eye in the plane is now on us—including Helen's beady, bloodshot ones.

"Oz…I'm sorry. I am. But, no, we simply don't have the time or resources to—"

I slam my hand against the cabin wall—and pull out my sat phone.

"Oh, really? Let's see how fast those resources dry up when word leaks to the press that HAC has started spreading to *people* now, too—and that Dr. Evan Freitas of the U.S. Department of Energy has been personally keeping that information under wraps!"

That's my trump card. I'm not bluffing, either. Hell, I'd give away the codes to the nuclear football if it meant saving Chloe and Eli. And Freitas knows it.

"Fine. But I have a better idea," he says at last. "I'll have the White House send a diplomatic security team from the embassy to find them. Your wife called your government satellite phone, right? That means we can track the location of the call. What would you do alone in Paris anyway, Oz? Let the highly trained men with guns save your family. You're a scientist. We need you in Idaho. To help save the *world*."

I'm steaming mad, but I have to admit, Freitas makes a compelling case. And short of barging into the cabin, there's not much else I can do to redirect our plane.

I slide my sat phone back into my pocket. All I can think about is how badly I want to see Chloe and Eli again. And "hold them in my arms."

CHAPTER 20

AS I HURRY DOWN the movable stairway that's been pushed up against our plane, I cover my mouth and nose with the collar of my shirt. A dust storm is brewing about ten miles away, and the air is starting to swirl with dust and grit.

A fleet of military and government vehicles is on the tarmac of Hill Air Force Base waiting for us: a few tan Jeeps, some black Suburbans, an ambulance, and a giant fluorescent yellow truck emblazoned with INL CRITICAL INCIDENT RESPONSE TEAM.

Sarah and our colleagues and I have barely stepped off the aircraft when a group of federal scientists wearing white full-body hazmat suits scamper aboard.

With Freitas directing them, they soon reemerge with Helen, strapped onto an upright wheeled gurney liked the kind used to transport Hannibal Lecter in *The Silence of the Lambs*. Except this one is covered with a clear plastic quarantine tent, and Helen is screaming and thrashing against her restraints worse than ever.

Even the stone-faced Marines there to protect us betray hints of fear.

After Helen is loaded into the rear of the hazmat truck, Freitas,

Sarah, and I are directed to the lead Suburban, where I'm surprised to see a familiar face.

"Look what the feral cats dragged in," says Mike Leahy, extending a meaty hand, the wind tousling his wavy silver hair. A high-ranking section chief with the National Security Agency, many months ago he acted as my unofficial government liaison and security escort. And let's just say…we didn't always get along.

I grimace as we shake hands. "Good to see you again, too, Mr. Leahy."

Our convoy is soon tearing down I-15, an endless two-lane desert highway, toward the laboratory. We *should* be able to see the Teton Range rising to the east, but it's obscured by that approaching dust storm.

"I'll be honest with you," Leahy says from the front seat. "When word started to spread back in DC that you were bringing back an infected human? It gave us quite a chuckle. But no one's laughing now."

"I'm glad," I say, "but you're wrong. 'Infected' implies some kind of disease-causing organism. Like bacteria, or a virus. We don't think that's the case here. Our working theory is, Helen's prehistoric-like behavior is somehow being triggered by pheromones, just like the animals' is."

"'Helen?'" Leahy scoffs. "You actually named that thing?"

"That *thing* is a human being," Sarah snaps. "With a *real* name we may never know. Show a little respect."

Damn. I'm liking Sarah more every day.

We ride in silence, and my mind immediately drifts back to Chloe and Eli. Freitas let me listen in as he called President Hardinson's chief of staff from the plane and got his personal guarantee he'd send a team to track down my wife and son in Paris. Now there's nothing else I can do but wait and pray that Chloe and Eli are found.

"That sandstorm sure is moving fast," says Sarah, gesturing out her window.

I look over—and my eyes nearly bug out of my head.

A smaller cloud of dust seems to be rolling across the desert right toward us.

"What…what in the hell…?" Leahy stutters.

As the cloud gets closer, I realize it's not a weather phenomenon at all.

It's a charging herd of wild mustangs. Dozens of them.

CHAPTER 21

"AW, SHIT!" LEAHY EXCLAIMS, grabbing his walkie-talkie. "Be advised, we got horses on our flank!" he barks into it. "All units—shoot and evade, shoot and evade!"

I hang on tight as our Marine driver slams the gas, and the entire convoy swerves off the highway and begins to speed up.

A mustang's top speed can reach over fifty miles per hour, but I'm confident we can outrun them. I feel even more hopeful as I watch other Marines in each of the escort Jeeps slide their M14s out their windows and unleash a torrent of automatic gunfire at the galloping broncos, quickly felling one after another.

But it's still too little, too late.

The remaining horses blast right through our line of vehicles. Glass shatters, metal groans, blood splatters, and bones crunch as thousands of pounds of car and horse collide at highway speed.

Two Jeeps, the ambulance, and one Suburban are toppled immediately, tumbling in different directions.

Then the Suburban I'm riding in is hit—and spins wildly, doing donuts in the desert dirt. Our driver, a female Marine, struggles to regain control as we're thrown around the car's interior like clothes inside a dryer.

"Go, damnit, go!" Leahy yells as the Marine pounds the accelerator, kicking up more dust behind us. He pulls her sidearm from her holster and fires frantically out the broken window at the mustangs as they regroup and charge again.

We can't get away fast enough. Neighing and snorting, the colts ram us again, head-on, with incredible force, first knocking the Suburban onto its side and then flipping it onto its roof.

Shattered glass rains down around me as I dangle upside down, pinned, suspended by my seat belt. Beside me, Sarah and Freitas are also hanging—it looks like the impact of the crash has knocked them both out cold.

I start to get woozy. Images of Chloe and Eli flash through my mind. If I'm dying, I definitely want those two to be my final thoughts.

My head flops over in the other direction. Through the dusty haze I can make out the yellow hazmat vehicle.

It's also been tipped over and is being pummeled just as mercilessly by multiple mustangs, its white-suited passengers as helpless as we are.

One of the horses manages to bash open the back doors—and the animal suddenly rears up on its hind legs in terror.

Helen is inside, still strapped to her gurney, but the plastic quarantine tent around her is badly torn, and she's screaming and baring her teeth at the horse.

Another mustang notices. Then another, then another. Before long, the colts have regrouped and are charging yet again—*away* from us.

The rest of the horses rejoin the fleeing pack and kick up another massive dust cloud in their wake.

CHAPTER 22

MY SNEAKERS AND RUBBER-TIPPED cane squeak against the floor as I hobble down this long, sterile hallway. I'm late to one of our frequent all-hands meetings, thanks to a pit stop at the lab's infirmary to grab a fresh handful of painkillers.

Over the past forty-eight hours, I've been popping those little guys like candy.

I push open the door of the conference room, which isn't easy. The stitches in my shoulder are still sore, and my busted knee still aches. Not to mention my three chipped teeth, sprained wrist, and the cuts and bruises over my whole body.

Seated around the giant marble table, their meeting already in progress, are Freitas, Sarah, Leahy, and most of the other scientists on our team. I say "most" because, between the feral human attack in the jungle and the mustang stampede on the highway, we've lost six colleagues in half as many days.

As I gently, painfully, sink into an empty chair, I have to remind myself how much worse my fate could have been.

Dr. Marilia Carvalho, a neuroscientist from São Paulo, is showing a series of colorful MRI brain scans on the large display screen. Since

When it finally settles, they're gone.

Wrecked vehicles and bloody horse limbs litter the desert ground. Human moaning wafts through the hot air, along with Helen's feral screams.

we arrived at the Idaho National Laboratory, we've been meeting like this often to share our research.

"But as you can see, while the subject's neurological structure is still identical to that of a typical human's, the vast majority of her neurological *activity* is occurring in the cerebellum, the medulla, and the basal ganglia."

"The so-called reptilian brain," Sarah offers. "An anatomical holdover from our days in the wild."

"Precisely. The higher capabilities in Helen's mind, like emotion and reason, have somehow been switched off. She most likely sees us modern humans as threats because her brain is literally functioning like a Neanderthal's."

"But why?" booms Leahy, jabbing his bulky arm cast in the air for emphasis. "That's the question Washington is paying you all to find out!"

"Our working theory is still pheromones, Mr. Leahy," says Freitas, who has two black eyes and a broken nose covered with a thick beige bandage. "We believe that explains why, as soon as the mustangs 'smelled' Helen, they backed off."

"But why is it happening to some folks and not others?" Leahy demands. "Why in some *places* and not others?"

Those are all fair questions. But I have an even more pressing one.

"Why hasn't it shown signs of regressing?" I ask. My colleagues all turn to me quizzically. "And why aren't any of you more afraid of that?

"Think back seven months ago," I continue, "when the president signed that emergency executive order, and all those world leaders joined her, putting a global moratorium on cellphone use, power generation, cars, planes. While it lasted, nearly all electromagnetic radiation was removed from the environment, and animal attacks plummeted—within *hours*. Wildlife started returning to normal."

Nods all around the table. Happy memories from a more hopeful time.

"But look at Helen. She's been in a completely sterile environment, inside a Faraday shield that blocks all electrical signals, for almost two days—and she's as feral as ever! We know how to reverse the effects of HAC on animals. But on people? We're back to square one. Is there an 'antidote,' or is it permanent? Shit, maybe it *is* contagious after all."

For what feels like forever, no one speaks. I'm not happy I just sucked all the air out of the conference room, but I said what I felt I had to.

"It's almost as if…some kind of irreversible physical changes are happening in Helen's brain," Sarah says somberly. "Perhaps we've been approaching it all wrong."

"Perhaps we should hear the latest on everyone's research first," Freitas says, steering the meeting back on track.

And so the rest of the scientists present their latest, equally inconclusive findings. Then the group starts filing out. We all have an enormous amount of work to do.

Shakily, I rise to my feet and begin limping toward the door. Freitas pulls me aside, placing a paternal hand on my back.

"Oz, I have some news," he says, his voice solemn. "About your family."

"The French cellphone number Chloe called from was identified, along with its last location: an abandoned monastery near Chantilly.

Apparently some kind of wacko animal rights cult has been squatting there."

I know right away they must be the "friends of the Earth" Chloe cryptically mentioned in her message.

"When agents arrived, the group itself was gone, but local police have some leads as to where they went next."

I can only pray Chloe and Eli are still with them. But I do have additional cause for hope. Among the other items they found in the monastery was our dog-eared copy of *A Tale of Two Cities*.

CHAPTER 23

"PLEASE HOLD FOR THE president of the United States."

I've met Marlena Hardinson many times before. I lectured her and other world leaders in the Cabinet Room of the White House. I even spent a few months living with her, the First Gentleman, and other high-ranking officials at Thule Air Base in Greenland after animals overran Washington and the government was temporarily evacuated.

Still, it's always pretty exciting to get a call from the leader of the free world.

Even when you know she's about to chew you out.

"Dr. Freitas, *Mr.* Oz," President Hardinson says pointedly as soon as she gets on the line, her husky voice brimming with frustration. "Can you please explain to me how an international operation costing over half a million dollars in travel, equipment, and logistical expenses *per day* has yielded no new breakthroughs on the animal crisis—or the growing *human* one—in almost four weeks?"

Freitas and I, along with just a few other colleagues (since most of our team, including Sarah, is still in Idaho hard at work), are back aboard our transport plane, this time flying across the Pacific. We're listening to this unexpected call on an encrypted speakerphone.

Freitas gulps, visibly rattled.

"I see you received the briefing packet we prepared for you, Madam President."

"Which might as well have been a stack of blank pages," she responds. "Except the part about the new human affliction being 'potentially irreversible.' Is that true?"

"We don't know for sure, ma'am," I cut in. "After all, we've only been able to examine one live specimen. That's why we're on our way to—"

"Tokyo. Yes, I'm aware. I spoke with Prime Minister Iwasaki this morning and informed him of your plans. He told me, in confidence, that there have been dozens of reported incidents involving feral humans in recent days, especially in the countryside."

"Have any been picked up yet by the Japanese press?" Freitas asks nervously. "Because if word gets out, we could be looking at a level of global pandemonium—"

"The prime minister, as *we* have, has been doing absolutely everything in his power to *suppress* any reporting on the feral humans. But if there's one thing I've learned after all my years in Washington, you can't keep a lid on bad news forever."

She's right. Especially of this magnitude. What was once just a silly rumor about bands of people "going native" in the game preserves of Africa has quickly proven to be a deadly reality all over, in places as diverse as Finland, South Korea, Egypt, and Japan. With most countries already teetering on the brink of anarchy, local governments have been trying desperately to sweep each incident under the rug. But it's only a matter of time before a cellphone video goes viral showing feral humans mauling innocent ones, and panic is unleashed around the world.

"Godspeed to you all," Hardinson says. "Oh, and Oz. My chief of staff informs me a security team in Paris has been making headway locating your wife and son?"

"Yes, ma'am," I reply. "Thank you again for all your administration's help."

"I'm not doing it out of the kindness of my heart, Oz. As I'm sure you know. We're only trying to save them because *you're* trying to save humankind."

I understand the president's veiled threat loud and clear: succeed, or else.

Seven billion lives are hanging in the balance.

Including the two I cherish most.

CHAPTER 24

OUR MITSUBISHI H-60 TRANSPORT helicopter thunders above the sprawling metropolis that is Tokyo. It's a stunningly dense city that seems to stretch on forever.

But even from such a high altitude, it's clear how badly the endless waves of animal attacks have ravaged Tokyo and its people.

It's midday, but judging by the lack of movement, it seems like huge swaths of the city are without power. Pillars of smoke dot the skyline. I can see flocks of striped sparrowhawks, ready to swoop down on human prey. Herds of something—wild boar?—flow through the streets like living, snorting rivers.

We bank southwest. Gradually the urban density becomes more suburban, then finally lush and mountainous. This tells me we're nearing our destination: semirural Yamanashi Prefecture, one of the most geographically secluded areas in the country.

Our chopper finally descends right in the middle of the main quad of Tsuru University, to the utter shock of the handful of students and faculty brave enough to be outside. Freitas slides open the cabin door and I see an elderly Japanese man hurrying toward us, shielding his face against the rotor wash. He has a bushy white goatee, thick black-rimmed glasses, and wears a tan suit and red bow tie.

My first thought is, the guy resembles a kooky mashup of Mr. Miyagi and Colonel Sanders. He must be Professor Junichi Tanaka, the highly regarded naturalist Freitas has been in contact with, who'll be leading us into the highlands to trap a second feral human.

Great. At least our guides back in South Africa were strapping young men. If we're attacked with Grandpa here at the helm? I'd say it's pretty much every man for himself.

"*Konnichiwa,* Freitas-*san,*" Tanaka says, offering a smile and his hand to shake. But Freitas has already started bowing and doesn't notice this. Tanaka returns the bow, just as Freitas rises up and extends *his* hand.

My boss is about to bow again when I grab his shoulder and stop him. Another time, another place, this little culture clash might be amusing. But not now.

"How about we ditch the formalities and get down to business?"

Freitas introduces the members of the skeleton team we've brought with us as Tanaka leads us all to an idling van. One of his graduate students, a twenty-something geeky-looking kid named Yusuke, is behind the wheel.

"First we will take you to the place where they killed all those Americans," Tanaka says, directing us inside the vehicle. "Then we will track them down."

"Uh...come again, mate?" asks Dr. Bret Clement, an immunologist from New Zealand, arching an eyebrow in concern.

This is rather alarming news to me, too.

"You told us there were only *sightings* of feral humans around here, Freitas," I say. "What American dead is he talking about?"

Freitas sighs and looks away. I know immediately he has once again kept his team partially in the dark.

"Mormon missionaries. About five of them. They'd been living in a remote mountain village near Otsuki. One afternoon, they were outside, apparently repairing their well. Neighbors heard screaming. By the time the cops arrived, they were all dead. Police sealed off the scene and claimed the deaths were a religion-motivated murder-suicide. The handful of neighbors who claimed they saw a pack of filthy, screeching Japanese rushing back into the woods? Their stories were deliberately disregarded and buried, by direct order from the Japanese Ministry of Justice."

Unbelievable. I supposed desperate times call for desperate, semi-illegal measures. But still. It's a miracle that word of the human attacks hasn't spread. Then again, the world is in such a state of chaos, maybe not.

Yusuke drives slowly and carefully along the narrow, winding roads that lead up the side of Mount Gangaharasuri, which I appreciate. But I'm mindful of how low the sun has slipped in the sky when we finally arrive at the missionaries' former village.

We exit the van, duck under the blue-and-white Japanese police crime scene tape, and do a quick walkabout of the property. The wooden home is modest, even by local standards. The stone path surrounding the well is covered with dried blood.

"My best guess," Professor Tanaka says, inspecting a topographical map on his iPhone and scanning the dense, hilly forest that starts just a few yards from the house, "is the pack went *that* way. The terrain is still steep, but less so. And in about twenty kilometers, there is a small cave beside a freshwater creek."

"The perfect spot for a prehistoric human settlement," Freitas says. "Let's go."

He starts marching toward the woods, but I hesitate. As do some of the others.

"Are you serious?" I say. "It's already after five o'clock. Sundown's in less than an hour. By the time we reach that cave, it'll be pitch black. Just think about that."

Tanaka answers instead. "Oz-*san,* there is a saying. *Jinsei ga hikari o tsukuru hozon shimasu.* Save a life, and your path will always have light."

"That's a nice proverb and all, Professor, but—"

"Proverb? No. I just made it up. Now let's go."

I can't help but scoff as Tanaka and Yusuke head bravely into the woods. Freitas and the other scientists soon follow. Reluctantly, I do as well.

I'm all for saving a life. Just as long as it doesn't cost my own.

CHAPTER 25

NIGHT FALLS ON MOUNT GANGAHARASURI. In addition to our guns and gear, each member of our ten-man team is using a long-range, super-bright LED tactical flashlight to illuminate the way. But as the last rays of reddish-orange sunlight disappear behind the horizon, a cold and heavy darkness engulfs us for miles.

"We are nearly at the cave," Tanaka says. With his eyes glued to the GPS program on his iPhone, he nearly trips on a hidden rock. "Just a few more kilometers."

"Good. And remember," Freitas says to the rest of us, "if those feral humans *are* there? You all know exactly what to do."

He means that we're to carry out the plan of attack we carefully crafted. We might not have learned much about what's *causing* humans to turn rabid yet, but we're certainly more prepared to sedate and capture one than we were outside Johannesburg. I'm feeling confident but also tingly with nerves.

Suddenly, Tanaka stops in his tracks. He holds up his palm for us to halt.

We all stand still as statues for a moment—until we hear a frantic rustling coming from some distant trees.

Instinctively, many of us, including myself, aim our flashlights in that direction. We can't see anything yet through the branches, but whatever it is, it looks to be about five or six feet tall. It's moving fast. And there's more than one.

Looks like the feral humans are coming for us first.

As we start to spread out and get ready, I slowly reach behind me. Slung over my shoulder are two weapons I can choose from: one lethal, one not. Even though it goes against our plan, my assault rifle is sounding pretty tempting right about now.

The rustling gets louder and louder…until four upright creatures burst from the trees and stagger toward us—not feral humans but Asiatic black bears.

Our group flies into chaos. Tanaka, Yusuke, Freitas, and the scientists all drop their flashlights, scramble for cover, and grope for their *real* weapons.

Thankfully, I already have mine aimed and ready.

I pepper the approaching bears with bullets as best I can in the darkness. I think I've hit at least two, but they keep coming. They roar and prepare to charge, their first target apparently Tanaka…

When just as suddenly, they all stop, retreat, and scamper back into the jungle, whimpering, their tiny tails literally between their legs.

"What the hell was that?" Freitas asks, picking himself up from the ground.

"Same thing that happened with the mustangs on the highway," I say. "Except this time, they didn't get a whiff of a feral human. Just a bunch of normal ones—who I guess should probably try to shower a little more regularly."

With relieved chuckles, our group reassembles and continues on.

We know we're getting close when we start to smell smoke from a campfire. Crouching low, we follow a tributary of the creek Tanaka mentioned. Before long, it leads us directly to the cave.

And inside, there they are.

CHAPTER 26

THERE ARE EIGHT OF them, all squatting in a circle around the glowing embers, feasting on what looks like barbecued squirrel. Their skin and tattered clothes are filthy, their posture apelike. Once again, they seem to eerily straddle the line between human and animal, modern and primitive.

We all spread out in a semicircle, take our positions…and quietly slip on gas masks. Then we each ready the miniature pellet guns we've brought, loaded with rounds of a custom-designed nerve gas containing a mild paralysis agent. To put it simply, our plan is to defeat the feral humans by not fighting them at all.

Freitas gives the signal and we each shoot our little pellets toward our unaware fellow *Homo sapiens*. The odorless gas should take just under thirty seconds to dissipate enough throughout the air, undetected, to begin making them woozy.

Instead, the humans' nostrils flare before the pellets even hit the ground.

Oh, shit, I think, as it suddenly dawns on me: the gas was designed to be odorless to *normal* people. These half-human/half-Neanderthals very likely have a superior olfactory sense. Or at least their brains do, subconsciously.

In which case, we're screwed.

Alerted to a disturbance, the feral humans look around, spot us, and let out a piercing battle cry. They leap to their feet, snatch up some of the prehistoric-looking weapons lying around the fire—spears, slingshots, tomahawks—and charge at us.

Freitas tries barking orders, but no one can hear him. And none of us cares. We're all scrambling to aim our weapons and stay alive.

One of them lunges at me with a "dagger" made of sharpened flint. She manages to slash my arm, but then I twist, parry, and shoot her in the chest point-blank.

More and more gunfire echoes across the mountain as our team fights back.

I can't see much of the "battlefield" through the fogged visor of my gas mask, but it seems like we've overwhelmed the feral humans with our modern firepower. Realizing they're outgunned, they actually start fleeing back into the jungle.

"You're not getting away that easy!" I shout, my voice muffled by my aspirator.

I pick the closest one to me—a middle-aged male—and charge after him. But he's fast and nimble as a cheetah and scrabbles up the rocky terrain with ease.

Realizing he's getting away, I make a risky decision. I stop running and kneel. I raise my rifle scope to my visor and try to line up the perfect, one-in-a-thousand shot, hoping to hit him in his leg and cripple him.

I squeeze the trigger—and yelp with joy as the man topples over into the brush.

I race over. Bleeding badly from his right thigh, he's now trying to *crawl* away.

But as soon as he sees me, the man stops and starts screeching and thrashing wildly, desperately struggling to punch and claw at me.

Even though he's wounded, watching his frenetic energy is still unnerving.

Which gives me an idea.

I take a few steps back, pull out my pellet gun again, and fire a little canister right at him. It bounces off him harmlessly and then begins releasing its paralyzing nerve gas. The man coughs and wheezes, kicks and writhes, but can't get away fast enough. Within seconds, he starts slowing down, finally collapsing on the jungle floor.

Satisfied that he's no longer a threat, I reapproach—this time readying the pair of handcuffs and leg shackles I've also brought.

I flip the unconscious man over, tug his arms behind his back, and slap on the cuffs, just like they do in the movies.

"You're under arrest," I can't help but say. "You have the right to remain human."

CHAPTER 27

"**WHAT THE HELL DO** you mean, her brain is *shrinking?*"

Freitas says it, but all of us are thinking it.

We're on our transport plane heading home to Idaho, in the midst of a heated video conference with Sarah, Dr. Carvalho, and the rest of our team back at the lab. Displayed on the other half of the monitor is the latest batch of MRI scans recently conducted on Helen's brain. And from the looks of it, her outer cerebral cortex isn't just inactive. Some of the tissue has actually started dying.

In feral *animals,* nothing like this has ever been seen before. Unless it's some kind of anomaly, it's a troubling development for all kinds of reasons—one giant one in particular.

It might mean whatever's happening to feral humans *can't be reversed.*

We know what's causing *animals* to go wild. And at least in theory, we know how to stop it. But Helen's been in electromagnetic isolation for a week and a half now, and her behavior has only gotten worse. And now her actual *brain* is wasting away? With more reports of rabid human attacks trickling in by the hour, from every corner of the globe, the number of possible permanent cases out there is staggering.

"That's why I think we need to change course," says Sarah, "and start working to find some kind of antidote. Or vaccine. Right away."

"Agreed," says Freitas. "This thing is spreading faster than any of us could have imagined. Before long, we could be talking about hundreds of thousands or maybe millions of infected humans—all lacking anatomically correct human brains."

"Don't be absurd," says Dr. Tanaka, who's flying with us to the United States to help handle the rabid Japanese man I captured in the jungle. "There is still so much about this affliction we do not know. To attempt to formulate a cure so prematurely is a reckless waste of time!"

Clearly Tanaka feels very passionately about this. I notice his brow is glistening, his cheeks are ruddy, and he's digging his nails deep into the faux-leather armrest.

But as the discussion continues, I can't help but zone out. For one thing, I'm exhausted. Trekking miles up the foothills of Mount Fuji and fighting off a pack of prehistoric humans can really take it out of you.

But I'm also a little light-headed with anticipation, a welcome change from dread. Because in less than twelve hours, I'll be seeing Eli and Chloe.

I got the call on my sat phone just as we were boarding in Tokyo. It came from a 202 number—a Washington, DC, area code—that I didn't recognize: the personal cellphone of President Hardinson's chief of staff.

"Mr. Oz, I wanted to tell you myself as soon as I heard. We found your family."

I nearly broke down and wept right there on the tarmac.

Diplomatic security agents, working with local French police, had tracked Chloe and Eli to an abandoned warehouse about forty miles outside of Paris, where they were hostages of the bizarre animal cult. My wife and son were rescued amid a shootout and put on the next plane out of there. Knowing that they're finally safe—it's indescribable. They'll be arriving at the Idaho National Laboratory just a few hours after we do.

Our video conference with the lab ends, but the debate over next steps rages on. Freitas and Tanaka are really starting to get into it. As for myself, I stifle a yawn. It's pitch-black over the Pacific and my eyelids are getting heavy.

"You'll all have to carry on without me," I tell them. "I'm gonna head down below for a little shut-eye."

I walk to the rear of our plane, toward the hatch that leads to the lower level, stuffed with our gear and equipment. I pass our captured Japanese feral human, Reiji. Tanaka had picked that name for him, explaining with a chuckle that it means "a well-mannered baby." The man is strapped to a gurney under a hard plastic shell like a newborn in an incubator, thrashing against his restraints like crazy. Watching him, I can appreciate the irony.

I'm about to head downstairs when I notice something about Reiji from this close up.

His brow is dripping with sweat. His cheeks are splotchy red. And he's shredding the thin mattress with his sharp-tipped fingers.

The sweat, the complexion, the nails—it's a more extreme version of everything I just saw Tanaka doing.

No...my God...does that mean...?

"Aaaaargh!"

CHAPTER 28

A VICIOUS ROAR COMES not from Reiji but from behind me. I spin around to the front of the cabin just in time to see Tanaka leap up from his seat and lunge at Freitas. Before Freitas can react, Tanaka's got his hands around his neck, nails digging deep into the flesh.

The other scientists, caught completely by surprise, scramble to yank the madman off, but he easily knocks them away with one hand, the other clutching Freitas's windpipe, blood gushing like a sprinkler. His sudden strength is incredible.

"Dr. Freitas!" I yell, dashing back up the aisle to help.

Tanaka turns around and sees me charging. He drops Freitas's limp body and rushes into the open cockpit—where our two pilots are just as stunned and even more helpless.

Tanaka grabs one of them from behind. In an instant he places her in a brutal chokehold and violently snaps her neck.

I'm just stepping over Freitas's writhing body, racing toward Tanaka, as he attacks the second pilot. While they tussle, Tanaka intentionally presses down the yoke with his knee—and the plane tilts into a steep nosedive.

I'm hurled forward and tumble around wildly. Everyone does—

along with an avalanche of loose papers and cellphones and laptops, each of the latter two now a deadly projectile.

Somehow I manage to get onto my hands and knees. Hanging on with all my might, I painstakingly crawl the rest of the way toward the cockpit, where Tanaka and the pilot are still fighting—and of course the feral human is winning.

Dizzy from the rapid altitude drop and throbbing with pain, I spot a fire extinguisher hanging by the cockpit door. *A weapon.*

I stagger to my feet, grab the heavy metal canister, and with every ounce of strength I can muster, swing it directly at Tanaka's skull.

Thunk. I can feel his cranium splinter. Tanaka cries out in pain, stumbles, but remains standing. "You bastard!" he shouts—as he turns to attack *me.*

I swing again. This time…I miss.

Tanaka springs toward me, but I crouch low and slip out of his grasp. Just as he spins back around, I take one more shot and nail him right in the middle of his face. His nose shatters, and three of his front teeth fall out of his mouth to the ground. Then he drops.

But my relief is brief. We're still plummeting toward the Pacific.

I yank on the yoke with trembling hands and desperately try to pull up. The plane levels off a bit, but I can feel we're still dropping fast. The instrument panel is blinking like a Christmas tree. Warning alarms are beeping wildly.

And both pilots are dead.

I have absolutely no idea what to do, except buckle in and pray.

I unbelt one of the pilots, shove him aside, take his bloody seat, and strap in.

I use all the strength I have left to keep tugging up on the yoke—especially when I see the dark, choppy water getting closer and closer. In my mind, I get glimpses of Chloe and Eli.

I can't die, I tell myself. *Not like this. Not without saying good-bye.*

And then, impact.

The noise is thunderous as the airplane smashes into the water. The cabin shudders and groans.

The plane finally comes to a stop. Almost immediately, I feel it start sinking.

Shaking off the stunned euphoria I'm feeling at having survived, I unbuckle my seat belt and stagger back into the cabin, which has been severed nearly in half and is quickly filling up with both water and smoke.

"Can anyone hear me?" I shout, coughing, wading through a flood of human carnage. "Is anyone okay?"

Silence. I can see that most of our team is dead, their bodies mangled and bloody.

But then, incredibly, I hear quiet mumbling. *Someone's still alive.*

Freitas!

"Hang in there, doc!" I say, splashing over to him. I sling the barely conscious man onto my shoulder. "We gotta get off this plane!"

I unlatch an emergency exit and a giant yellow slide-raft automatically inflates and extends into the water. *Thank God.* I put Freitas onto it, then give the sinking cabin a final look.

I see Tanaka floating facedown. Reiji, too, is long gone. His gurney is on its side, the plastic covering is shattered, and a giant shard has decapitated him.

Damnit—after all that. So much for bringing either of *them* back to the lab.

But there's no time for wallowing. I climb into the raft myself, disconnect it from the plane, and we immediately start to drift away in the choppy current.

I've barely gotten Freitas rolled onto his back so I can examine his wounds when, with a final, awful groan, our burning aircraft splits in two and disappears underwater.

CHAPTER 29

QUICK: HOW LONG CAN the average person last without water? A week? Five days? Three?

It's one of those scary stats you've heard a hundred times but never thought you'd need—until you find yourself floating on a raft in the middle of the Pacific.

I couldn't tell you how many hours it's been since the crash. If I had to guess, only about eighteen or so. But they've been long. And hellish.

Throughout the cold, pitch-black night, I tried to stabilize Freitas and stop his bleeding, ripping strips of fabric from our clothes to make crude bandages and tourniquets.

As the sun came up, I got a clearer view of his injuries. Mine, too. But when morning turned to afternoon, the sun's rays turned hot and punishing. With nothing at all to use for shade, our skin quickly started to burn.

I still had my satellite phone in my pocket, but it had been smashed to pieces. I thought about trying to paddle—with just my hands; why didn't they put oars on this thing?—but had no idea which direction to go. I figured it was better to save my strength anyway. *And* stay close to the crash site. I mean, a military transport plane on a critical government mission just crashed into the sea. Surely *somebody* saw that on the radar and sent help.

Right?

Now it's night again. The temperature is dropping. Salt is crusted around my eyes. My mouth feels like sandpaper, my skin like it's on fire. Freitas is slipping in and out of consciousness again. He's still breathing, but barely.

Having hardly slept in three days now, I feel the gentle bobbing of the raft start to lull me to sleep. I know I should keep my eyes open, to monitor Freitas, to keep watch for a passing ship to flag down. But I feel so weak. Bone-tired.

I think again of Chloe and Eli, who I pray have made it safely to the Idaho lab by now. And I know I have to keep going, keep fighting. They need me. The *world* needs me, I think, feeling myself start to drift off. *To survive dozens of animal and feral human attacks on land, only to die on the open water…*

The blare of a foghorn startles me awake.

It's just before dawn; the sky is an incandescent blue. I don't see anything in front of me. Painfully, I turn around—and behold a glorious sight.

A gray navy destroyer, off in the distance, steaming our way.

"Dr. Freitas!" I exclaim, gently shaking him awake. "They're coming! We're saved!"

He groans in acknowledgment. And I think I detect the tiniest smile on his bruised, bloody face.

A black Zodiac raft is soon lowered from the destroyer into the water. It speeds toward us, carrying about eight men in dark-blue camouflage uniforms. A few of them are wearing white armbands bearing a red cross: medics.

The highest-ranking sailor calls to me as they get near: "Are you Jackson Oz?"

"Yes!" I croak. "And I'm all right. But Dr. Freitas is in serious condition. The rest of our team…and our specimen…*both* of them… they're dead."

Their boat comes to a stop near our yellow raft. Medics quickly rush aboard, carrying a stretcher over to Freitas. "You're safe now," the officer tells me.

Am I? I wonder, as I'm wrapped in a silver thermal blanket and guided onto their craft. Twenty-four hours ago, I witnessed a seemingly normal human being turn into an unrecognizable beast. Without explanation. Without warning.

We speed back toward the looming destroyer, bouncing up and down in the waves, the cool ocean mist spraying my face.

As I glance around at all these young sailors, I can't help but wonder: Could any of them be next? Could their commanding officer? Could Freitas?

Could I?

CHAPTER 30

JOINT BASE PEARL HARBOR-HICKAM. In 1941, it was the site of one of the most devastating surprises in American history.

Across all the main islands of Hawaii, wild animal attacks are as bad as anywhere. But there have been exactly zero feral *human* ones. Ever.

At least that's the word from Captain Paul Fileri, the stern, buzz-cut commander of the vessel that rescued me. My de facto escort since we arrived on base, he's standing next to my bed in the infirmary as a nurse drains my wounds and changes the dressings.

"That's good news," I say, adding, "or I suppose it is. But what I *really* want to know—"

"You *suppose?*" Fileri asks, almost offended. "Oz, a third of the president's Animal Crisis Task Force—from what I understand, the leading international experts in this matter—was just killed. The team leader is down the hall in a medically induced coma. Maybe you don't quite grasp the severity of the situation, but—"

"With all due respect, Captain," I say, clearly irking this career military officer who isn't used to being interrupted, "I've devoted *years* of my life to this 'situation.' I've traveled to every corner of the globe looking for answers. Shit, I just captured one feral human in the wild, then killed a second with my bare hands! So I think I grasp its 'severity' very well, thank you. But right now, all I care about is my family. Are they all right? Please. Tell me. Did they arrive safely in Idaho?"

Fileri frowns. "I don't know anything about that. My orders came directly from the Pentagon, as soon as they learned your plane had gone down. Full-steam to its last known position, rescue any survivors, bring them back to base—"

"I understand that. And I'm very grateful. But what I'd be even *more* grateful for right now is an encrypted satellite phone."

Fileri's eyes narrow. So I explain.

"To speak to the White House. They're expecting my call. To tell me, now that Freitas is out of commission, how the *commander in chief* would like us to proceed."

As I'd hoped, those were the magic words.

Even if they were a big fat lie.

Of course I'll try to get ahold of somebody close to the president, maybe her chief of staff again, to find out how I'm supposed to get back to the rest of the team running the show now, and what the hell we're supposed to do next.

But obviously my first call is going to be to the Idaho National Laboratory.

Captain Fileri exits the room. He reappears a few minutes later with a bulky black wireless phone, promising to check in on me again shortly.

As soon as he's gone, I tap the arm of the friendly nurse still tending to me. "Sorry, I know you're busy, but you must have a smartphone on you, right?"

Thankfully, she does. Even more thankfully, cell service on the island is still working. Within seconds she's done me a huge favor: she's googled the Idaho lab's main number. I can't dial it fast enough.

It rings.

"Come on, pick up," I whisper under my breath.

The line rings again. Then again.

I'm bursting with anticipation now. I can't stand it.

Another ring. Then another.

By the eighth ring, my cautious excitement has been replaced by a sinking feeling in the pit of my stomach.

I'm calling the main switchboard, in the middle of a workday, at a major federal scientific facility. There should be someone there to answer the damn phone!

CHAPTER 31

"SHE'S COMING! RUN!"

Clutching Eli in her arms, Chloe follows the command without question as screams and gunshots ring out nearby.

She quickly falls into step with a stream of other scientists and lab personnel all racing down a long corridor tinged with the smell of smoke.

Running for their lives.

All across the biological sciences wing, red lights are flashing and a shrill alarm is blaring. The warning system was designed to be used if a poisonous chemical or deadly pathogen was accidentally released into the air.

Today it's sounding for an even more terrifying reason.

A feral human being—captured in South Africa and brought here for study, nicknamed "Helen"—has just escaped.

The chaos began only minutes ago. As a distracted researcher was preparing to conduct a brain biopsy on her, Helen somehow managed to swipe a scalpel off the instrument tray, cut through her restraints—then slice open the scientist's jugular vein.

A rabid woman on the loose with a surgical blade would be scary enough. But Helen is scary *clever,* too. When armed guards charged into the research lab, she leapt out from a hiding spot, overpowered one, stole his pistol, and gunned down the rest. Then she took to stalking the halls, shooting at anyone and everyone she saw.

Chloe can feel her heart thudding in her chest. Eli is crying and clutching onto her tight. People are pushing and shoving. It's chaos.

And the smoke and gunshots are getting closer.

Chloe had first heard rumors while she was still living as a virtual prisoner among those freakish cult members in France that the animal affliction had begun spreading to people. Given her science background and all she knew about HAC, she dismissed it as utter nonsense, scientifically impossible. Just more of their crazy ranting.

But soon after she and Eli were rescued by American security forces and put on a plane to be reunited with her husband, she learned that Oz was on his way back from Japan, where he'd just captured a feral human.

Suddenly it didn't sound so crazy after all.

Chloe rounds a corner, which leads to an indoor courtyard of sorts, one that branches off into four separate corridors.

The scientists scramble every which way, but Chloe wants to be smart. She wants to run to an exit—not run in circles. She's only been at the lab for a few days and doesn't know her way around. Standing paralyzed, she debates where to go…

"Chloe, this way!" A familiar voice.

Dr. Sarah Lipchitz—a young biologist Chloe met when they first arrived. She'd tried to bond with Chloe over their shared "love" of Oz. At first Chloe was put off by this younger, perhaps prettier, woman who wouldn't shut up about how wonderful her husband was. Of course Chloe believed that Oz had remained faithful, and it was clear that Sarah was just feeling sad and lonely and scared. Chloe had begun to warm up to her.

And thank God she did. That woman might just save their lives.

With Sarah in the lead, the group dashes down the center-left hallway. Sure enough, they soon spot a bright red EXIT sign above a door that clearly leads outside.

Suddenly, a bullet streaks by and ricochets off the wall, just inches from Chloe's head.

She screams and glances behind her. Helen must be looking for a way out, too: half-screaming in some African language, half-roaring in rage, she's coming up behind them!

"Keep running, don't stop!" Sarah urges. Chloe runs, pulling Eli at her side.

They finally reach the exit and burst outside into the hot desert evening.

"One of the Jeeps!" Sarah yells. "They leave the keys in the ignition. Go, go!"

The women and Eli scurry over the asphalt in a parking lot filled with official laboratory vehicles. They make it to one of several tan SUVs. Sure enough, it's unlocked.

They all pile inside: Sarah behind the wheel, Chloe in the front seat, holding Eli on her lap.

Helen, still running after them, fires twice more—shattering the rear windshield—as Sarah starts the engine and burns rubber.

The Jeep is heading straight for a metal checkpoint gate that is both unmanned and closed tight. They're picking up speed—but so is Helen.

Right above those ominous little words OBJECTS IN MIRROR ARE CLOSER THAN THEY APPEAR, Chloe sees the feral woman starting to sprint—fast enough to leave Usain Bolt in the dust. She's gaining on them.

"Now what?" Chloe shouts. "We're trapped!"

Sarah keeps the pedal to the floor. "Just hang on!"

At the very last second, she cuts the wheel away from the checkpoint and the Jeep barrels straight through the chain-link fence.

At least they've made it out of the burning facility, but Helen has, too.

She continues chasing them, getting terrifyingly close. She fires the last few bullets in her pistol, striking the back bumper and popping a rear tire. The Jeep keeps going, picking up more and more speed, Sarah finally putting some real distance between them.

Chloe spins around in her seat just in time to watch the feral human reach a point of frustration and slow down—then abruptly change course and run instead toward the vast desert surrounding the blazing, smoking lab.

"*Mon dieu!*" is all Chloe can whisper in relief. Panting heavily, her pulse racing, she adds, "*Merci,* Sarah. You saved us."

The two women trade a look and glance back at Helen. She's already disappeared into the dry expanse.

CHAPTER 32

AFTER FAILING TO REACH a single soul inside the Idaho lab, I've started freaking out. A *lot*. It seems more and more likely that something awful may have happened there.

And that Chloe and Eli might be in danger. *Again*.

So I change tack. Googling the number on the iPhone the nurse lent me, I call the Department of Energy's main switchboard. Finally I speak to a human being…in media affairs. All he'll tell me is that, yes, there's been a recent "incident" at the lab and "multiple persons are still unaccounted for."

Unaccounted for? Not what a guy wants to hear when he's three thousand miles and half an ocean away, and his wife and son might be involved.

"Get dressed, Mr. Oz," says Captain Fileri, marching back into my room. He tosses me a pair of sneakers, khakis, and a blue button-down to replace the flimsy hospital gown I'm wearing. "We're wheels up in thirty minutes."

Fileri explains he's just spoken with the White House. Despite the recent loss of nearly two-thirds of the Animal Crisis Task Force scientists, Washington is scrambling to keep the team's critical work moving forward. They're assembling a whole *new* group of experts, and they're ordering me to return to DC via military plane to be among them. Immediately.

"That all sounds fine and dandy, Captain," I say, "right after we make a quick pit stop to pick up my—"

"That's a negative," Fileri snaps. "The command is to evac you and Dr. Freitas off the island and back to the capital. No detour, no delay. There just isn't time."

It's very clear to me that the captain isn't going to budge on this. I know he's just following orders. And I know the country—the world—still does need my expertise.

But I also know that Chloe and Eli need me more. And the last time I put my work ahead of my family, I nearly lost them forever. I am *never* going to do it again.

So I put on my best poker face and say: "All right, sir. I'll be ready in a minute."

As soon as Fileri leaves, the clock starts ticking.

For me to make my escape.

CHAPTER 33

I THROW ON THE fresh clothes, grab my still-damp wallet from the meager personal effects on the table, pocket the iPhone (sorry, nurse!), and quietly lock the door to my room. Then I hobble over to the window.

I pry off one of the wooden boards meant to keep out animals and see I'm on the third floor—way too high to risk jumping down safely.

So I decide to do what I've seen in old movies so many times. I'll use my bed linens to make a rope.

Nuts, I know, but what other choice do I have?

I strip the bed and hastily knot two sheets together as tight as I can. I tie one end to the railing, toss the other end outside, and carefully start to climb down.

I'm about halfway down when, damnit, one of the sheets rips.

I fall into some bushes, intentionally rolling and tumbling to soften the impact of the fall. I may be a little scuffed up, as if I wasn't already, but I've made it.

Now I just have to slip aboard the next commercial flight to the mainland…just as soon as I figure out where the hell the airport is.

I search in Google Maps, but the screen doesn't move. I try again. Still nothing. Seriously?

But then I hear a loud rumbling overhead—and see a jetliner flying dangerously close to the ground. Is it going to crash? No. It's coming in for a landing. Which means the military facility and the airport are just blocks apart.

Keeping an eye out for both wild animals and military police, I race across the base. A lot of the chain-link fence along its perimeter looks damaged by—what else?—attacks from feral creatures, so I find an opening, slip through, and keep running as fast as I can until I reach the airport. It's not hard to find it, since hundreds, maybe thousands, of people are cramming into the terminal, desperate to get off the islands. Which won't be easy. Since the animal crisis has dragged on, the number of flights all around the world has gone down dramatically, while the cost of flying has skyrocketed.

I get in a long ticket line and wait. I'm terrified that any second, Captain Fileri will burst through the doors and drag me back to the base.

Finally it's my turn to speak to an agent. I breathlessly explain my situation and how badly I need to get to Salt Lake City—the closest major city to the lab—to make sure my wife and son are okay.

But the agent barely lets me finish. The next available direct flight to anywhere in the Rockies, she tells me, isn't for four days.

My heart sinks. My eyes tear up. I beg and plead. Isn't there *any* other option?

The agent purses her lips and types rapidly. Maybe I've gotten through to her.

"There's a plane leaving for Vancouver in twenty minutes, if you can make it. From there you can connect to San Francisco. Then to Chicago. Then double back through Phoenix to Salt Lake. You'll be traveling for over thirty-six hours straight but—"

"I'll take it!" I exclaim, slapping a credit card down on the counter. By some miracle, my cards were undamaged in my wallet.

And I need all *three* of my credit cards to split up and cover the whopping price: $29,487. Insane, but worth every penny.

The agent hands me my ticket and I take off like a rocket through the packed terminal. I somehow manage to make it through security and reach the gate seconds before the boarding doors close.

CHAPTER 34

I SCREAM IN TERROR as I'm jolted awake in my seat—and grab the unfamiliar hand just inches from my throat.

But then I relax and let it go. And turn beet-red from embarrassment.

It was just the flight attendant tapping me on the shoulder, asking me to bring my seat to the upright position. We'll be landing soon in Salt Lake City.

The past forty-plus hours have been a blur of exhaustion, stress, and actual pain. The meds I was given at the military hospital in Hawaii have long since worn off, and my entire body is throbbing. Add to that multiple layovers and multiple delays in multiple airports, each more chaotic than the next…plus the constant threat of a feral human attack at any moment and…well, you get the idea. Not exactly a pleasure trip.

Seeing all the other passengers whip out their smartphones after we landed in Vancouver, it dawned on me. I felt so stupid for not thinking of it sooner. My wife doesn't have a cell I can call, but of course I still know her email address.

Using the nurse's iPhone, I logged into my personal account for the first time in weeks and fired off a quick note, praying that Chloe would think to check her email, too.

About six hours later, when I landed in San Francisco...no response.

But then, *another* six hours later, after we touched down in Chicago...I dabbed away tears of joy at the sight of my wife's name in my inbox. Still more tears came as I read about the terror that went down at the lab and their harrowing escape.

As soon as the plane's wheels make contact with the tarmac and my journey finally ends, I leap up out of my seat, race down the jet bridge, sprint through the busy terminal, and burst outside into the hot Utah afternoon.

The curbside pickup area is total mayhem. Cars honking, cops shouting.

My iPhone died hours ago, before I could arrange any kind of specific meet-up time and location with Chloe. I need to charge it, badly, but first I want to find some ground transportation. I've come so far, and my family is *still* so far.

Then something catches my eye: a handmade sign with the words JACKSON OZ.

It's being held up by Chloe, standing in front of a tan Jeep as if she were a chauffeur, a megawatt smile plastered across her beautiful face.

Eli is clinging to her leg. "Daddy!" he yells, letting go and bounding up to me.

He leaps into my arms. I squeeze the boy so tightly I'm afraid he might pop. Covering his messy hair with kisses, I carry him to Chloe and wrap her in the hug as well.

And the three of us just stay like that. Half-laughing, half-crying. No words. Just unimaginable relief.

And infinite love.

Finally we pull apart, sniffling, wiping our eyes.

"So, how was your little vacation, *mon amour?*" she asks with her trademark smirk. I've missed that so much. To answer, I give her a long, deep kiss.

The front door of the Jeep opens and out steps Sarah. Like my wife and son, she looks tired and stressed and grimy but also relieved to see me. The feeling is mutual, especially since Chloe told me in her email that Sarah helped save their lives.

"I don't know how to thank you," I say as we embrace.

"*I* do," Sarah answers, pulling away to look at both Chloe and me. "No more crazy expeditions to far-flung corners of the globe. No more unnecessary tests. No more big government agencies telling us what to do. And no more delay."

Chloe understands where Sarah's going with this and picks up the thread.

"*Oui!* Feral human attacks are on the rise. And with the president's task force in ruins…yes, we will need equipment and a laboratory and new specimens…but the three of us—working *together* this time, Oz—may be the best shot the world has at finding a cure."

I smile, feeling a real sense of hope and optimism I haven't in weeks.

"I couldn't agree more. And I think I know where we should start."

CHAPTER 35

NOTHING LIKE FLYING FORTY hours on five different planes, then taking a six-hour road trip through the sweltering Nevada desert.

But, hey, I'm not complaining. I'm alert and fired up and feeling great. I've got my wife by my side, my little boy dozing in the backseat, and the beginnings of some actual working theories about the feral humans and how to cure them.

"I agree with you, Oz," says Sarah, "that the pheromones that feral humans give off must be different from normal humans'. When animals get one whiff, they all go running. But how do you explain the tissue death we saw in Helen's brain? Pheromones affect behavior, mating, aggression. Not brain damage. It's impossible."

"Actually, it is not," Chloe offers. "Research has shown that cells can die in response to pheromones if response pathways are lacking."

"Fine," Sarah concedes. "But the more pressing question is, how do we stop it? And reverse it in the people already affected? How in the world do we regrow human brains?"

"Easy," I reply. "Stem cells. They're like cellular free spaces. With the potential to grow into any kind of cells in the human body—including brain tissue, as long as we program them right. Toss in a high-octane antihistamine to block pheromone absorption, and we'll be in business!"

Chloe and Sarah consider my suggestion, both clearly intrigued by it.

"We all know stem cell therapy is still a new field," I continue. "The idea I'm proposing is radical. It's hard. But—"

"You're wrong, Oz," Sarah replies. "It's simple. It's elegant. It's… genius."

Chloe chuckles good-naturedly. "Careful now, Sarah," she says. "My husband's head is full of great ideas. But we don't want it to get so big it explodes."

We continue driving down this long, deserted stretch of I-15. Dirt and shrubs are all around us, as far as the eye can see. A highway sign says we're only about seventy miles out from our destination: Las Vegas. An old friend of Sarah's from grad school is an adjunct professor of biochemistry at the University of Nevada. With his expertise—not to mention the use of his lab space and equipment—we just might be able to pull off my "genius" idea. Emphasis on *might*.

"Of course, the *real* challenge," Sarah says, "is going to be finding some feral human test subjects. If history is any guide, that won't be—"

"Oz, look out!" Chloe shouts.

Before I have time to react, a pack of rabid coyotes lying in wait along the highway shoulder leap up to the road—easily a dozen or more, all yipping madly—and onto the Jeep.

I swerve wildly—to try to shake them off, since none of us has a weapon, and because I can't see a damn thing.

The animals scratch at the windshield like fiends. They snap their razor-sharp fangs at the shut windows. The smart little bastards even claw at the tires to try to pop them and slow us down.

Trying to kill us.

Eli is crying. Sarah is screaming. Chloe is just hanging on for dear life.

Me, I keep jerking the wheel side to side, accelerating fast and then braking sharply, trying desperately to shake them off.

And it seems to be working. One by one the coyotes lose their grip and tumble off onto the hot asphalt. So I keep it up.

Until I *mess* it up.

There's a highway sign I don't see until it's too late.

I sideswipe it. Direct hit. The passenger window next to Sarah shatters.

The Jeep goes spinning wildly out of control.

Most of the coyotes are thrown off, but once our car comes to a helpless stop, they regroup and charge at us. I stomp the pedal, but it's too late.

At the broken window, I see two coyotes approach to leap in…

But instead of piling inside, they begin howling.

They jump away from the car just as fast and scurry away. Within seconds, the entire pack has disappeared into the desert.

Jesus, another close call! All that talk about rabid humans, it's easy to forget there are still *animals* out there who want us dead just as much.

Slowly Chloe, Sarah, and I all catch our breath. We're relieved. We're safe.

But then, we begin to trade nervous glances.

Sarah is turning pale with shock. We're all having the same chilling thought.

The reason the coyotes ran away the second before they jumped through Sarah's window...

Is because she must be on the verge of going feral.

CHAPTER 36

UP UNTIL NOW, THE stakes of the feral human crisis had been huge but impersonal.

I knew thousands of people around the world had been affected, but I didn't *know* any of them. Helen and Reiji were total strangers to me. I'd only met Tanaka a day before our fateful flight over the Pacific.

But now, with Sarah about to join their ranks, this damn plague has come to my doorstep. She's a colleague. A friend. A good person who saved Chloe and Eli's lives at the Idaho lab. A good scientist whose help we need to discover a cure.

"But she could kill us, all of us!" Chloe anxiously whispered to me the first night we spent inside the UNLV lab. "If she *changes* before we discover the antidote—"

"Incentive for us to discover it even faster," I replied. "And on the bright side, now we have a rabid human guinea pig to test it on."

I tried to downplay my wife's fears, but of course I felt them tenfold.

I shared with her, Sarah, and Dr. David Stapf—Sarah's biochemist friend from grad school—what I saw happen to Tanaka in the minutes before he went rabid. I wanted us all to be on the lookout for similar warning signs: sweaty brow, red face, clenched fists, arguing, and aggressive behavior.

And just in case we miss them somehow, Sarah's given us permission, if she starts acting dangerously, to put her down. Like an animal.

I respect her bravery, but, God, do I hope it doesn't come to that.

Except now, it's looking like it might.

We're wrapping up day six locked in the bowels of the University of Nevada science complex, trying to program the stem cell genetic sequence that will bring dead white blood cells back to life in a petri dish. So far, we've crammed about two months of research into one grueling week. And I feel it. My back aches from hunching over my microscope eighteen hours a day. My eyelids are heavy, my mind foggy.

I glance over at Eli, on the floor in the corner, playing with a collection of lab equipment serving as toys. Rubber gloves, plastic funnels, safety goggles. Just watching his innocent smile is enough to keep me going.

Next I look over at Chloe, working furiously at her lab station, pipetting solutions into test tubes. Her dedication makes me love her even more.

Then I notice Sarah, also working hard…but with more intensity somehow, almost with an anger in her eyes. Could this be the first sign of aggressive behavior? I watch as she subtly dabs some sweat off her forehead. It's hot and stuffy down in this lab; I'm sweating, too. But maybe that's another symptom of her impending change?

"You guys, check this out!" David exclaims, leaping off his lab stool.

Chloe, Sarah, and I head over and take turns peering into David's digital microscope.

"Oh my God," Sarah says, seeing it first.

"Incredible," Chloe adds after she looks.

Finally, it's my turn—but I don't have any words. Just silent joy.

I'm watching thousands of previously dead white blood cells regenerate right before my eyes! I clap David on the back with excitement.

"Amazing, right?" he says. "Obviously there's no way to know if this nucleotide chain will have the same effect inside a feral human brain. I *think* it should, but—"

"David," I say, "we don't have time to 'think.' We need certainty. Now."

Chloe suggests we share our results with the new DOE team, with whom we've been in sporadic touch the past few days, so they can run with it themselves.

"For sure," I say. "But first, get these stem cells into a nasal spray canister. When Sarah starts…transforming…at least we'll have *something* to try on her."

Everyone soberly agrees, and David eagerly sets to work. We all do. That was just the kind of moral boost we needed. Maybe we'll cure this thing after all.

But then, barely two hours later, everything changes.

Every single light and device and computer in our lab flickers off.

"Incroyable!" Chloe shouts, enraged. "We are on the brink of saving mankind and we lose electricity?"

"It's all right, honey. Relax. I'm sure it's just…"

In the near distance, we can hear glass being shattered. Guns being fired. And humans screaming, grunting, roaring.

Feral humans.

We all immediately realize we're no longer safe here.

I turn to David. "How many nasal injector serums did you make?"

"Just…just one," he stutters. "For Sarah."

Great.

"Make sure you bring it," I say. "I have an awful feeling we're going to need it."

CHAPTER 37

ALL FIVE OF US—Chloe, Eli, Sarah, David, and myself—race up the stairs and outside. It's the first time we've stepped foot out of the lab in days. The sun is setting and the mostly empty campus is bathed in eerie, shadowy orange light. *Only* eerie, shadowy orange light. It looks like the entire school has lost power.

Scratch that. Glancing around in every direction, I see that the blackout stretches across *the entire city of Las Vegas*.

I also see the source of those feral war cries.

A band of rabid humans is stalking across the campus—a dozen, at least, maybe more, chasing and ferociously attacking everyone they encounter. They're also a distorted reflection of Vegas society. One is wearing the black vest and green visor of a blackjack dealer. Another, the heavy makeup and skimpy dress of a cocktail waitress or maybe a prostitute. Another is a Vegas cop, in uniform, firing his sidearm.

"What do we do?" asks Sarah, panicking.

The truth is, I have no goddamn idea.

We can't just stand here, but we don't have a plan, either. We don't have a new safe destination. And we don't have any weapons.

All we've got is a wrecked government Jeep with a quarter tank of gas. A single nasal injector with an antidote that *might* work. And each other.

The most important thing of all.

"What do we do? We run!"

Scooping up my son and pulling my wife along by the hand, we rush to the Jeep still parked not far from the lab entrance. We pile inside and peel out.

By the time we get off campus, we spot another cluster of feral humans coming from the other direction—the Strip, its famous casinos and hotels all scarily dark. One of them wears the uniform of a hotel housekeeper. Another, a burly bald man wielding a shotgun, has on the shiny black suit of a casino bouncer.

They catch sight of our speeding Jeep and decide to pursue. As they pick up speed, the bouncer fires at us, spiderwebbing our rear windshield with buckshot.

"Go faster, Oz!" Chloe shouts from the backseat.

So I do. And soon we're whizzing down one of the city's wide boulevards, littered with trash and abandoned cars and the occasional non-feral person running for his or her life.

We seem to have lost the second pack of rabid humans, but more keep popping up around every corner. A Chinese tourist hurls a concrete cinder-block at us with incredible strength, leaving a divot in the hood. Even a feral Elvis impersonator leaps in front of the Jeep and bashes one of the headlights with a baseball bat.

"*Merde!*" Chloe exclaims. "Goddamn you, Oz! I said faster! Why can't you ever do anything right?"

"Hey, I'm trying my best here!" I call back to her, almost more freaked out by her angry tone of voice than by the rabid humans we're trying to avoid.

When I suddenly realize…holy shit…

I turn around in my seat to look at Chloe. Her forehead is drenched. Her cheeks are deep crimson. She's holding Eli in her lap, but clutching onto him so tightly that his skin his turning white—and she's digging her nails into his flesh a bit, making him cry.

Please. God, no…it can't be…

Chloe lets loose a bloodcurdling primal roar and grabs me from behind.

She—not Sarah—is the one who's been going feral!

Our car fills with screaming and mayhem as Chloe attacks me like a maniac, clawing at my face and neck from behind, quickly drawing blood.

Stunned, Sarah and David scramble to yank her off while I try to keep the car moving and under control. We swerve wildly—sideswiping a telephone pole, scraping the roof of an overturned tour bus, just narrowly avoiding being hit by a flaming Molotov cocktail hurled by a feral human on a rooftop I can't even see.

As the fight continues—me resisting and struggling and gurgling on my own blood—I see David pull the nasal injector from his pocket. He rips off the cap with his teeth, yanks Chloe's head back by her hair, jams the injector up her nostril, and depresses the trigger.

Chloe gasps and screams. She starts to writhe and seize, shaking horribly and frothing at the mouth. It's an awful, agonizing sight…

But it's over in just a few seconds.

Chloe releases her grip on me and slumps back in her seat. Slowly, her breathing and complexion return to normal. Her muscles relax.

Before our eyes, *she becomes a healthy human being again!*

"What…what just…did I…?" is all she can manage to croak.

"It's okay, Chloe," I whisper, tears of relief streaming down my bloodied face.

Sarah, David, little Eli—they're overwhelmed as well.

I refocus on the road ahead. I press down on the gas even harder and squeal onto a highway on-ramp.

Behind me, through my rearview mirror as we drive farther and farther away, I can see columns of smoke rising. Sin City's been turned into a war zone.

But at least we saved my wife.

And thanks to our antidote, *we might save humanity, too.*

"It's okay, baby," I say again. "Everything's going to be okay."

EPILOGUE

"AS OF TODAY, MADAM PRESIDENT, the vaccination rate stands at seventy-three percent. That includes all major urban populations of one million or more—"

"What about the *remaining* twenty-seven percent of Americans, Dr. Freitas?"

President Hardinson glares at Freitas, who's one of the many advisors, military leaders, and scientists—Chloe and I among them—seated around this giant polished conference table. He gulps.

"We're working on it, ma'am."

He can say *that* again.

Over the past three months since we developed the antihistamine antidote to human pheromonal rabidity, or HPR, as I've dubbed it, in that musty Las Vegas lab, I've been helping the government mass-produce and disseminate it as quickly and widely as possible. Given the strained state of the country—and the world—the progress we've made has been remarkable, even for a cynic like yours truly.

But I hear the president's concern loud and clear. A quarter of the country has yet to be inoculated.

That's eighty million new potential feral humans. A staggering thought.

Clearly we have our work cut out for us.

The meeting of the newly re-formed and renamed Animal & Human Crisis Task Force ends, and Chloe and I start to leave. We find ourselves exiting alongside Freitas, who's pushing himself along in his wheelchair. The plane crash left his face badly scarred, and he's still too weak to walk—but he's alive, miraculously.

"Chloe, Oz, I meant to ask you both," he says. "How are you finding the accommodations?"

"This isn't the first time we've lived in seclusion with the leader of the free world," I say. Just a few weeks ago, the White House was evacuated for the second time in eight months. The threat of feral human attacks was just too great. "It ain't the Ritz," I continue. "But living underground sure beats living in the Arctic."

Chloe and I walk down one of the mountain compound's long, dim central hallways toward the daycare center. Eli now spends most of his waking hours there, learning and playing with kids his own age—instead of being alone with his frazzled parents or running away from animal attacks or witnessing his mother turn feral. We've only been at Raven Rock a few weeks, but already the kid is thriving. Which warms my heart. And gives me hope.

But as we near the daycare center, I can tell that there's something on Chloe's mind. I stop walking and take her hand. I stare deep into her gorgeous eyes.

"What is it, Chloe?" I ask tenderly.

She avoids my gaze and gently runs a finger along one of the deep scars on the side of my neck—a mark from when, just a few months ago inside that Jeep in Vegas, she tried to kill me. She's still upset about the whole episode, even though I've tried to convince her it wasn't her fault. And that I still love her more than anything.

"I don't know," she answers softly. "I am just…afraid. HPR is under control. All three of us are together again. We're living in the safest place on Earth. And yet…I don't know how to describe it. It's just a feeling. An uneasy one."

I pull my sweet, beautiful wife into a warm embrace. "I know," I say. "I'm afraid, too. But there's nothing to be…"

I stop talking—because I hear something.

A faint, distant *scratching* sound. Almost a burrowing. But it's not coming from one particular spot. It's emanating, almost echoing, all around us.

Chloe and I share a look. We both hear it. We're both concerned.

And then, we're both shocked—as *a swarm of cockroaches emerges from the cinder-block walls all around us,* pushing through every nook and cranny, thousands of them, black and shiny, squirming and wiggling…

And coming right at us.

ABOUT THE AUTHORS

JAMES PATTERSON has written more bestsellers and created more enduring fictional characters than any other novelist writing today. He lives in Florida with his family.

MAX DiLALLO is a novelist, playwright, and screenwriter. He lives in Los Angeles.

MICHAEL BENNETT FACES HIS TOUGHEST CASE YET....

Detective Michael Bennett is called to the scene after a man plunges to his death outside a trendy Manhattan hotel—but the man's fingerprints are traced to a pilot who was killed in Iraq years ago.

Will Bennett discover the truth?

Or will he become tangled in a web of government secrets instead?

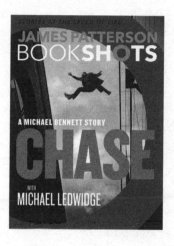

Read the new action-packed Michael Bennett story, out on August 2, available only in

CAN A LITTLE BLACK DRESS CHANGE EVERYTHING?

Divorced magazine editor Jane Avery is content with spending her nights alone—until she finds the Dress. Suddenly she's surrendering to dark desires, and New York City has become her erotic playground. But what begins as a sultry fantasy has gone too far....

And her next conquest could be her last.

Check out the steamy cliffhanger *Little Black Dress,* out on July 5, available only in

BOOK**SHOTS**

LOOKING TO FALL IN LOVE IN JUST ONE NIGHT?

INTRODUCING BOOKSHOTS FLAMES:

original romances presented by James Patterson that fit into your busy life.

FEATURING LOVE STORIES BY:

New York Times bestselling author Jen McLaughlin

New York Times bestselling author Samantha Towle

USA Today bestselling author Erin Knightley

Elizabeth Hayley

Jessica Linden

Codi Gary

Laurie Horowitz

…and many others!

AVAILABLE BEGINNING JULY 2016

SHE NEVER EXPECTED TO FALL IN LOVE WITH A COWBOY....

Rodeo king Tanner Callen isn't looking to be tied down anytime soon. When he sees Madeline Harper at a local honky-tonk—even though everything about her screams New York City—he brings out every trick in his playbook to take her home.

But soon he learns that he doesn't just want her for a night.

Instead, he hopes for forever.

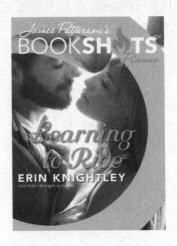

Read the heartwarming new romance, *Learning to Ride*, coming soon from